AMONG US

AMONG US

Jacqueline Druga

PRESS

VULPINE
PRESS

Published by Vulpine Press in the United Kingdom in 2025

Cover by Claire Wood

ISBN: 978-1-83919-622-5

www.vulpine-press.com

Also by Jacqueline Druga:

What we Become

Like many, Mackenzie Garret complains about the weather. It is the hottest summer anyone can remember. The high temperatures are out of control with no end in sight. Until it all changes.

Overnight, blue skies become gray, and the hot, hu-mid weather turns to rain, then snow, then ice as the temperature plummets.

The entire northern half of the country is thrown into chaos as blow by blow, storm after storm, nature rips into the world, tearing it apart. Towns and cities are evacuated, and Mac and her family are forced to leave their world behind and face a treacher-ous journey south to safety.

Omnicide

A town practically cut off from the rest of the country, Griffin is always the last to know about everything. Fax is the most reliable method of communication and the local newspaper is the main source of outside information.

When a freak car accident occurs on the outside of town, no one thinks much of it. That is until deer are found sick and cov-ered in an unusual growth, and they lose contact with the next town.

Cut off and isolated from the rest of the world, Griffin is un-aware of the threat growing outside the safety of their little town. One that could endanger their entire existence.

FIRST PHASE

ONE
THE KITCHEN

This isn't one of those stories or movies, where the teenager comes in, says what they want, and saves the day.

That's what I wanted to say to my oldest son as he stood by the kitchen window, staring out, drinking his orange, whatever it was, in that glass.

It went through my mind watching him in the after moments of an argument he had with his father.

A stupid argument. One that shouldn't have happened and one that sent my husband storming out of the house. Calvin was a police officer in our small town. Always on Route 8, on traffic enforcement, and when he was in a bad mood, I felt bad for the driver with a bad inspection sticker.

Damn it, Sam. If he pulls Mr. Mosely over again for that crack in the windshield, I won't be happy.

To be fair, my husband wasn't a bad cop, his mood dictated how many people he pulled over. Then usually in traffic court, he'd say, 'Let them go. Drop it.'

Except for Mr. Mosely.

My husband didn't budge when it came to him.

The dumb argument between father and son, played in my head. It wasn't how I wanted to start my day, especially before heading to work. The way Sam spoke, with his 'yeah, rights' and 'whatevers' went round and round in my mind.

"Does this day feel weird to you?" Sam said, staring out the window and interrupting my cyclical train of thought. "Just a weird energy."

"Sam, this isn't one of those young people movies where a young person can say what they want to an adult and all of the sudden, wow, they're smart and everyone older listens."

Sam choked as he took a drink, laughing. "What? What are you talking about? That has nothing to do with what I just said."

"I know. But you know what I'm talking about." I stood and walked over to him, grabbed his glass and sniffed it. "What is this?"

"It's my powder drink. Better than breakfast."

"It stinks like old shoes."

"Ma."

I handed it back and went back to my seat at the table and my coffee.

"I didn't appreciate your tone with your father. I know you're all into those shows and books where teenagers are the heroes, and they say what they want to adults—"

"No, that's not me. I don't read. I read but not like Jake. That's Jake."

"Whatever."

Another shake of his head and Sam finished his drink. "Where is this coming from?"

"Again, I'll say it. Your tone with Dad."

"He was wrong."

"He's your father."

"He's wrong."

"You're seventeen years old."

"And that mitigates the fact that he's wrong?" Sam asked.

"I don't think that's the word you're looking for."

"What?" Sam questioned.

"Mitigates. You mean negates."

"Same difference."

"Ha." I laughed. "No. Not even close."

"Why do you always have to make me feel so dumb?"

"Oh, stop it," I said.

Sam was in one of those moods. Argumentative, arrogant, such as my oldest son. He didn't know the meaning of 'biting his tongue'.

"What does this movie and book thing have to do with my fight with Dad?" Sam asked. "And it wasn't a fight. I was right."

"Be that as it may."

Sam chuckled as he sat down. "What does that even mean?"

"Why do I feel this conversation is going in circles?"

"Mum." He sighed. "He was being shitty—"

"*Language.*"

"Okay, sorry. He was being nasty to me."

I nodded. "I get it. But he's your dad. He's older, and even though I one hundred percent agree that parking the car mid-driveway keeps it shaded, he wants it near the garage. It's his car. You borrowed it. He pays for it."

"We'll never see eye to eye."

I stared at my oldest son. A spitting image of his father in a younger way. The wavy brown hair that had that cowlick in the front. I remembered his father when he was seventeen. Cal had the same hair, only he wore it puffier.

Calvin had the same attitude; he never wanted to admit he was wrong, and he had to have his way.

Granted, I got my way more than he did. But I was smart enough to let him think he got his way even when he didn't.

Except with the boys and their names.

I wanted to name the kids something original, biblical, or even after grandparents, but Calvin wanted names that were short, sharp, and tough, with one syllable nicknames. I gave into him on that; I know a losing battle when I see one.

Although to be honest I never thought I'd have three boys.

Now, I had one just like my husband, which is why they butted heads so much. My middle son, Jake, was like me, and Luke, my nine-year-old…we were still trying to figure him out.

"Are we done fighting?" asked Sam.

"We're not fighting. I just don't like when you're mouthy with Dad; there are other ways to handle it other than acting like a character from a young adult novel."

"Which character and which novel?" Jake asked as he entered the room.

Sam held out his hand in a point to Jake. "See. *He* reads."

"I don't know which novel or character." I shrugged. "I just meant in general. I'm comparing Sam to one because he was fighting with dad again. Every movie I watch with a teen hero, they always seem to say what they want."

"Ah." Jake nodded and walked to the fridge. "That's because they want a young audience."

"So, young people want to see other young people telling off adults?" I asked.

"No," Jake replied. "They like to see their voices are heard. Sam is nothing like the teen novel and movie heroes."

Sam grinned. "Thanks."

I did a double take and looked at Sam. He didn't get that his younger brother wasn't paying him a compliment.

Luke continued, as he pulled out the milk. "Him and Dad will always fight. And always over something stupid. It's not disrespectful. It's genetics."

"Thanks, little brother," Sam said.

"It's disrespectful," I said.

"He just needs to rephrase," Jake said, grabbing cereal and a bowl.

Such a difference between the boys. Jake was two years younger than Sam, yet in so many ways was more mature.

"Like Mom," Jake sat down. "She wins every argument with Dad because she knows how to verbally run him off the road. Speaking of running. Is it today?"

"Yes," Sam replied with a shiver to his voice, then moved his hand across his belly. "The scout is supposed to come today. Maybe that's why this day feels so weird."

"Yeah, it does," Luke said. "Like a strange energy."

"Exactly." Sam snapped his finger.

"It's nerves. You're feeling the nervous energy." I closed my eyes. Just thinking about it made my stomach fill with butterflies.

"You're going to do great. I know it. This is it. I am getting out of the store early to be there."

"Are you sure?" Sam asked. "I mean, I want you there. You can tell me honestly how I did."

"Yes," I replied. "I want to be there. And you're going to do great. I'll pick up Luke and…" I turned my head. "Where's your brother?"

Jake answered, "He was up. I just saw him. He should be down."

Just as Jake said that, my youngest, Luke, entered.

"There he is," I said. "Luke, did you want cereal?"

Luke didn't answer. He walked straight into the kitchen and instead of to the sink or refrigerator like he always did, he walked to directly to toward the pantry.

No emotion, no words. In a stride that didn't break, he walked right into the closed door.

Sam and Jake thought it was funny.

"Dude, it's not open," Sam said.

"You sleepwalking?" Jake joked.

"Luke?" I called his name.

Luke stepped back, stared at the door and walked forward again.

I jumped up. "Luke? It's not funny."

As if he didn't hear me or was in some sort of trance, a few inches from the pantry, Luke revved back his head as if doing some sort of head banging dance, and slammed it into the door.

"Luke!" I shouted.

Bam.

He slammed it again.

6

Bam.

Then again.

He kept doing it. Faster and harder.

It was so unexpected, so quick and shocking, it was hard to react.

"Luke, stop!" I screamed, leaping forward but Sam was faster than me, making it to Luke as the door to the pantry cracked with the force of the hit.

There was blood everywhere. On my son, on the door.

Sam wrapped his arms around Luke, pulling him back.

Then as if my nine-year-old had some sort of super strength, he lunged forward, out of Sam's grip and into the door.

Sam tried to grab him, but wasn't fast enough.

This time, Luke hit so hard, he bounced back, straight as a board, and falling backwards like a tree.

I screamed for Jake to call for help, as I dropped to the floor to help Luke.

Everything that occurred happened in a span of no more than forty seconds.

I held my youngest on the floor, a kitchen towel to his bleeding head, confused and scared.

What happened?

What was wrong with my son?

TWO
OUT OF THE BLUE

"Seizure," the doctor said with confidence.

We stood outside the emergency treatment room, and I peeked through the window. Luke lay on a bed, hooked to IVs, oxygen and monitors. He sported a bandage after getting fifteen stitches in his forehead.

Bringing my arms tighter to my body, I nodded in acceptance of what the doctor was telling me.

Not Cal.

One thing about being in a town of three thousand was that when any emergency call came through, the entire first responder team heard it.

Cal arrived back at the house right after the ambulance pulled in.

He arrived as Luke woke back up, fought with Sam, and tried to get up.

When the doctor said seizure, my husband, as if some sort of medical guru, shook his head.

"Nope. A seizure? Really? Out of the blue."

"They can happen out of the blue."

"That isn't it."

The doctor looked nearly offended by my husband's rejection of his diagnosis. "Officer Doyle, I assure you, it was a seizure."

"And I am pretty damned certain you're missing something," Cal said. "A nine-year-old boy bangs his head into the wall over and over and it's a seizure? No. It's something else."

"Like?" the doctor asked.

"Did you check for a tumor?'

"We scanned. Everything is good."

"Drugs?"

"Cal," I scolded. "He's nine."

"Still." Cal looked at the doctor.

"I doubt it was drugs but we are waiting on toxicology," the doctor said. "It is a seizure. Actually, they're called psychomotor seizures."

"So, you did an EEG?"

"An EEG will only show abnormalities *during* a seizure."

"It doesn't feel right," Cal said and looked at me. "Shelby, it doesn't feel right."

"Mr. and Mrs. Doyle," the doctor said. "This is my initial diagnosis, when Luke wakes up, we'll run more tests. Until then, we have him sedated so he isn't at further risk should another seizure occur. All that said, there is a possibility that it may not be a *physical* condition causing this."

I gasped. "Do you think he's possessed?"

Both men looked at me like I'd just personally offended them both.

"Shel," my husband said with a scolding tone. "Jesus, you watch too many movies."

"While we can't rule anything out," the doctor said calmly. "I can confidently say it's not demonic possession."

Not that I believed it, but to witness what my son had done that morning was beyond bizarre.

"I'm going to go talk to Sam and Jake," I said. "I'll be back."

I grabbed my husband's arm as I walked by him, and his hand draped over mine.

"He'll be fine," Cal said. "I feel it."

I wished I could have said that I did too, but I couldn't. I was so unsure of what was happening, I could only nod as I walked away.

When I stepped into the waiting room, both of my sons stood and rushed towards me.

"He's stable," I told them. "They believe he was having seizures."

In the same fashion as his father, Sam stepped back, shaking his head in disbelief.

"This wasn't a seizure."

"They say it was," I replied. "Psycho something seizure."

"Like he's insane?" Jake asked.

"Mom, he looked possessed," Sam stated.

"I said the same thing," I replied. "But Dad and the doctor looked at me like I was crazy."

Sam stared at me. "Something is off."

"I know." I glanced down at my watch. "Why don't you boys go to school. Take my car." I reached into my purse for the keys.

Sam shook his head. "We can't leave."

"Yeah, you can. Go to school. You have that big meet," I told him.

Sam lowered his head, shaking it slowly back and forth. "How can I run when my brother is on my mind?"

"Exactly," I told him. "You run for your brother." I grabbed his hand, placing the key in it. "Go. I will keep you posted and hopefully, I'll be there."

As I watched my older sons relent to my request and leave, a part of me felt foolish.

Were things so bad, so bizarre, as I had believed?

There is always a part of you that feels that maybe you're just overreacting. I felt as if I'd been so dramatic, I was a little embarrassed, and was certain I was overplaying it all. Even as my youngest lay unconscious in a hospital bed.

After watching my two older sons reluctantly agree and leave for the high school, I returned to the emergency department.

My husband was inside the room, standing by Luke's bed.

They told us it wouldn't be long before they moved him up to the pediatric floor. But I wished he would wake up before then.

Just give me something Luke, even the smallest sign that you'll wake up.

Was he unconscious because he did damage to his head? What did they sedate him with?

"I can wait here," I told Cal. "Go back to work."

"No. Nope." He shook his head. "I'm not leaving until I know something. This is just the oddest thing."

"I know." I reached down grabbing Luke's hand. "Our poor baby."

"Did you call into the store?"

I nodded. "They understood. Although Barron is stuck in the 1950s or something."

"What did he say now?"

"That old line about staying home and just letting you work."

Cal shook his head. "I don't know where he gets this from, he's like what twenty-three."

"His grandfather. Just like he got the job."

"Old mind said," Cal said. "And, this is a small town, we're already decades behind. Besides, you like that job."

"Great gossip." I smiled, then looked down when I felt Luke grip my hand. "Luke?"

"Mommy?" He opened his eyes. "Mommy, where am I?"

"You're in the hospital, baby, but you're okay," I told him, as if I believed it.

"Why?"

"You hit your head."

I saw the look of confusion on Luke's face.

Cal leaned down to him. "Son, what do you remember?"

"Jake telling me to hurry up. I was getting dressed."

"That's it?" I asked.

Luke nodded.

I glanced to my husband, and in my mind, I figured we were both wrong. Maybe it was seizures. Really, what else could it be?

As the minutes passed, Luke became chattier. So much so, I wondered if they were going to send him home. But the doctor insisted they keep him and watch him.

Since he showed marked signs of improvement, Cal went to catch a few hours of work. He promised to return so I could make Sam's track meet.

It didn't take long for them to move Luke to a room. By that point he was pretty hungry, so they fed him Jell-O and broth, to keep him going while he had some more tests done.

By two in the afternoon, my son was exhausted and starving. Cal swooped in like a hero, bringing his son a cheeseburger and milkshake.

With Luke feeling better, I felt confident in leaving to go to Sam's track meet. He seemed normal, almost as if nothing had even happened. The doctors were going to bring a specialist in the next day to chart a course of action, and possibly prescribe some medication to control future seizures.

It was scary, watching Luke do all that without any control of his actions. It caused *me* to feel out of control. I couldn't help him or protect him. That was a horrible feeling.

After saying goodbye, I kissed and hugged him, telling him I would let him know how Sam did with his meet.

I really did feel all right about leaving him.

He was fine now.

But he and that experience were never far from my mind.

Forgetting I had given my car to the boys, I had to walk to the high school; thankfully it wasn't that far from the hospital.

I arrived as the runners were walking on the field. I took my usual spot, in the corner of the stands, out of Sam's eyeline so he didn't get nervous.

Jake was closer to the field, in the stands with all his friends. Sam waved to him, not me, but that was fine. He never did.

He knew I was there; I was sure of that.

In fact, Jake was the only one Sam looked at when he stepped onto that field., He didn't look in the stands. I knew why. He didn't want it to seem like he was searching for the scout.

But I looked around those who were there, trying to spot the scout myself. I hoped, for Sam's sake, he really had shown up. I knew from what the coach said, that the scout was a man, an older one, and from what I saw there were only three in the stands.

One of them had to be him.

We all cheered a little louder, clapped a little longer, but Sam didn't need that. He did great.

Fantastic.

I was so proud of him. He did great in the hundred-meter dash and long distance, finishing first. I wanted to run down to the field to congratulate him, but I knew there was still one final relay.

I caught Sam looking my way, finding me in my hiding spot. I waved and gave him a thumbs up.

A day that started out *so* bad was taking a turn for the best.

Bright sunny sky, perfect weather, a great event for my oldest.

All that changed with the blink of lights.

Just as the final relay came to a close, I made my way down the bleachers and saw the flashing lights of the police car.

No siren, just flashing lights, racing our way.

The squad car pulled to the field and Cal stepped out, leaving the door open.

At first, I thought he was making some grand entrance for Sam, but I got this twitch in my stomach when I saw my husband's face.

Something was wrong.

Very wrong.

With my heart beating out of control, my throat closing up, a feeling a dread swept over me and I ran his way with rubbery legs.

"Cal?" I said breathlessly.

"Get in the car, Shel. We gotta go. We're losing him."

I barely got a 'what' out, when he hurriedly ushered me into the car, slammed the door, jumped in and took off with the lights and sirens blasting.

I looked over my shoulder back at the field, my sons were standing there watching.

We didn't say anything to them.

Nothing.

He just rushed me away.

"What's going on?" I asked. "What happened?"

"I don't know. I just had to come get you before…" He choked on his words.

"Before?" A thump hit my stomach. "Oh God."

Cal pulled up to the hospital and we both jumped out.

I didn't even think he turned the car off.

He grabbed my arms, running with me, never telling me what it was, but I didn't need to be psychic to know.

Cal pressed the elevator button repeatedly as if it would make it suddenly come, then with a grab to my arm, he rushed me to the stairs and we ran up the two floors.

I was not one to physically exert myself, yet I took those steps like a champion, never once losing my breath.

It felt surreal. I knew something was wrong, yet I couldn't stop myself from thinking Cal had to be mistaken, as if I were wishing that to be true.

We ran down the hall.

The last I saw Luke, he was sitting up, laughing, eating a cheeseburger and drinking his shake.

As we arrived at the room, I saw the two nurses slowly walking out.

I couldn't breathe. I knew before I even stepped into that room what I was going to see.

The doctor's back was facing us and he turned around, exposing my son.

Luke lay flat on his back, arms to the side, the blankets were off of him. No wires were attached, no IV.

More horrifying than that was seeing my youngest son, my baby, without color.

"I'm sorry," the doctor said to us. "I'm so sorry."

THREE
To the Core

The loss of my child was beyond devastating. How does one even begin to go on? I knew I had my oldest sons, but a part of me felt that wasn't enough.

I wanted to die.

In the first few hours, the pain was so tremendous I screamed out for God to take me. Just take me.

He didn't. Not yet.

There was the initial shock at the hospital. It wasn't real. He was sleeping. He'd wake up. There had to have been a mistake.

But there was no mistaking the feeling of my son's lifeless hand, cold in mine.

After Cal and the boys said goodbye, I sat for hours waiting for Luke to wake up. Praying for a miracle that never came.

The room was dark, the sun had set, and in my grief, I forgot that I wasn't the only one suffering and in pain.

No one rushed me to leave, they didn't.

I finally relented and kissed my baby goodbye, allowing them to take him from the room after a nurse came in.

She said to me, "I know the pain. I've been there. I am sorry for what your family is going through."

My family.

My children lost a brother and one other person felt the same as me.

Cal.

He lost a child as well.

As hard as it was, I left that room and sought out my family. They were patiently waiting for me.

We went home in silence and, after taking a sedative, I wept to sleep that night.

I didn't know how I was going to make it through the funeral, let alone the arrangements.

It was hard because they were doing an autopsy. I tried not to think about that.

Cal handled most of the arrangements, I was useless.

I couldn't wrap my head around it. My son who was never sick a day in his life, the picture of health, one minute is knocking himself unconscious, the next laughing, the next gone.

While I hated the fact that they were doing an autopsy, I needed to know what took my child.

It delayed everything which ended up being a blessing.

A week to mentally prepare for the funeral.

I gained some strength in that week. The shock had worn off and I kept it together through the viewing and service.

Sam and Jake were amazing. I knew they were filled with so much sadness, but they were pillars of strength for me and Cal.

Cal tried to be strong, but he was breaking.

He took a leave of absence from work, and I was glad for that.

Barron, my manager at the grocery store, told me to take all the time I needed and assured me that I'd always have a job there.

Funny thing was, a part of me just wanted to go to the store and work.

Take my mind off of things.

Everywhere I looked I was reminded of Luke and what we had lost.

As hard as funerals are, there is something to be said about the ritualistic nature of them. It wasn't a new thing, burial services had been around for thousands of years, if not longer.

They were a sense of closure.

The ending to a book, a book I loved, that had come to a close.

It was amazing how many people brought food to the house. The vast majority of it started arriving right before the viewing. I swore we would have enough food for weeks. Yet, at the after-funeral-luncheon, I worried that we didn't have enough to feed everyone.

So many people showed up for the funeral and lunch. Family members I hadn't seen in years, friends from high school. Even though it wasn't, it felt like half the town made an appearance at one point.

I kept it together. Cal did as well.

But I needed a break. Just a short one.

All those people in my house, eating, talking, looking at me with pity.

Mrs. Mosely brought over something called sherry. I thought it was only for cooking, but she said to sip it.

I poured a tiny glass, stole a cigarette from my Uncle Charles and, after telling Cal, I retreated to the bedroom.

"Just come and get me in fifteen," I told him. "I just need a few minutes."

He fully understood and I vowed to make it up to him when I could.

Upstairs, I moved the dressing chair close to the window and lit up, blowing the smoke out there. I looked to the backyard, the swing set that was barely used.

I was crushed and confused. There were no answers. No yet.

Lifting the screen on the window, I put out the cigarette on the exterior windowsill. And though I knew I was supposed to sip, I downed the rest of the sherry and stood.

As I reached to move the chair, a single knock came at the door, and Cal stepped inside.

"I'm coming," I told him.

"That's not why I'm here." Cal stepped aside, opening the door wider and Todd Rose stepped in.

Everyone in town knew Todd Rose. Star quarterback at Hawthorne High twenty years earlier. Then went on to be the star reporter at the *New York Times*, and he was slated to be a big deal until he went overseas to cover a conflict. He was injured, left to walk with a cane. Shell shocked, he came home and saved the local paper.

He was still a reporter, nice guy or not.

Why was he in my bedroom?

"Todd needs to talk to you," Cal said.

"Mrs. Doyle." He walked toward me. "I am very sorry for your loss."

"Thank you, but why are you here?" I asked. "Wait." I held up my hand. "That was rude, I'm sorry. You came to pay your respects."

"I wish it was just that." Todd nodded to Cal and Cal closed the door. "I know, by talking to Officer Doyle, that you are confused on what happened. I hope to maybe give you some answers that you may not otherwise get."

"I don't know what you're talking about," I replied.

"You know I worked for The Times, right?"

"Everyone does."

"I still have connections there and in DC. I was talking to a source who was trying to get a story to The Times. When I heard, I…I was grateful we live in this small town. Isolated, right, and then I heard about Luke."

Cal exhaled loudly. "You have to hear this, Shel, sit down."

"No, I'll stand."

"We don't have proof." Todd lifted his hands. "I'll get it. But I don't think we'll need proof at this rate."

"What are you talking about?"

"I don't believe it was a seizure that took your son's life," Todd said. "My source says it's a virus."

"A virus?" I asked shocked. "Surely, the hospital would know."

Todd shook his head. "Pretty sure they don't. Or didn't. When Luke passed, there were a few dozen kids hit with the same thing. Odd behavior, banging heads, death within hours."

"So, he's not the only one," I said.

"Far from it now. The reason I came over is to tell you before any news breaks. I'm trying to get it to break. I talked to my source right before I came over. She is with the CDC. You know what that is?"

"Of course."

"As of this afternoon there are thirty-two thousand children that have lost their lives here in American to this. Thirty-two thousand, the same as Luke, all under thirteen."

Hearing that took my breath away. I stumbled back and sat on the bed. Thirty-two thousand mothers were feeling what I was feeling.

A virus.

"Those numbers are huge," Cal said. "Huge."

"Okay, so if there is that many," I questioned. "Why isn't this out? I would think the bigger news source, would be reporting it."

"They don't want it out," said Todd.

"Why?" I asked.

"Because it's not just a virus," Todd stated. "They think it was an attack. A biological weapon."

"Are we at war?" I asked.

"If we aren't, after this," Cal said. "We are now."

Slowly, I shook my head.

"But with whom?"

FOUR
CHAOTIC MINDS

"Russia, it has to be Russia." The argumentative man in the really horrible suit, sat on a panel on television pointing at another man. "Who else has those capabilities?"

"Just about any country with a scientist," the other man retorted.

Click.

With the aim of the remote, I shut off the television.

To the dismay of my sons, they groaned and yelled.

"No," I told them. "Dad said we watch together at night. He doesn't want you on this twenty-four seven."

"The news is only on twenty-four seven when something happens," Sam argued. "Besides, what else is there to do?"

"Chores maybe," I suggested.

Jake did a double take at me. "Mom, where are you going?"

"Back to work. The store is only open for eight hours. It's A through D today." I wagged my finger at Sam. "Don't forget to come down and get the food. Bring your license. Daddy left money on the kitchen counter. If you don't pick up today, we have to wait until next week."

"I don't understand how it works." Sam stood. "I just go in, show my license, and they give me stuff?"

"No, you can shop, but certain items are limited to one per order."

"Can I bring Jake?"

I nodded. "Yes, but just be diligent about trouble. Barron said last week there were some fights. Be ready for some long lines."

"When should I go, early or late?"

"I'd wait for an hour or so after we open. They won't run out; they're enforcing," I said.

"I don't understand why you're going back to work," Sam said.

"For the same reason you hate not having school. Working will help me keep my mind off of things. Besides it's been four weeks. I need to."

Jake paced across the living room, shaking his head. "So much is going on, so fast. It's like a movie only worse. It's real."

I walked to Jake, placing my hand on his cheek. "I know."

We were living the reality of it, the first wave of the virus or weapon. There was a huge debate in the political and scientific community. Was it a biological weapon or was it just nature saying it was time to clear population?

It had been four weeks since I lost my son. Four weeks of stopping as I passed his room. Glancing in with an abundance of heartache. Catching the scene of him that remained.

In the course of four weeks, the world turned upside down.

There was no denying something was going on: children, all younger than thirteen, were coming down with this virus. A form of bacterial encephalitis, whether man-made or not.

At first, when it struck Luke, it was selective. A few others, dozens, as Todd had said.

Then within days the numbers grow. Now as we entered week four, it was in the millions.

There was no rhyme or reason for it, no indication that it was contagious, which was the main argument that it was a weapon.

On the flip side of that, a weapon would hit all at once, not gradual.

Honestly, I didn't care. It already affected me and my family. We now were like millions of others.

Saint Mary's started a support group in town. The population of three thousand had dwindled as we seem to be burying dozens of our own a week.

All that caused an understandable chaos.

More than I thought cried out that it was the end of the world. That God's end was near, taking all the children first. But how and why? My son suffered. If it was God's end, and he was taking the children, why make them suffer? Surely, God was all powerful enough to snap his fingers and they'd disappear.

No, it was something more than that.

It was every novel about a virus ever written rolled into one.

Next step was society falling apart and I was going to be smack dab in the middle of it working at Eagle Mart.

Two weeks earlier, before my return, the government began strictly enforcing a seldom enforced hoarding law.

Hearing it so much on the news, I knew it by heart. US Code 4512 – Hoarding of designated Scarce materials. Everything was scarce. No one wanted to work, truck drivers were being hijacked on the roads, supply and demand were way off balance. The law went into effect in 1951 and here were now, abiding by it.

Cal hated it.

He went from traffic officer to enforcement officer. Working the lines at the store the following up on tips the station received about people stockpiling.

They gave people a choice, face charges or allow them to seize the goods.

What had we become? So fast, we fell apart. Our tight-knit community went from sharing hot dogs and laughs at Community Day, to turning their neighbors in over having too much food.

How did these people find out someone near them was hoarding? Were they told? Did they spy?

We didn't have much at all, if we did, I wouldn't say anything. There was no one you could trust. Then again, I wouldn't hoard. I was not one to break the law. I followed the rules, after all, I was married to a police officer and he surely, at least as far as I knew, followed the letter of the law. Even the new ones.

I walked to the store because Sam would need the car for our weekly allotted shopping time. It wasn't too far and it gave me time to think.

The streets were quiet, with very little traffic. Businesses were still open, but signs on the doors indicated they were short staffed and not all items were available.

I arrived at the grocery store fifteen minutes before my shift, and had to go in through the back. A line had formed outside that spanned an entire block.

When I went in, I could hear the television playing. Barron had it on in the break room and those who were working were watching. He stood there, arms crossed against his lanky body. His hair was neatly combed and he even wore a tie. He looked surprisingly together for the hectic day ahead of us.

"Welcome back," Barron said.

His welcome was repeated by nearly everyone in the break room.

"Thanks." I saw my timecard and punched it. "Anything new?"

"Congress is trying to pass a law requiring all children under thirteen to be tested."

"For what?" I asked. "Last I heard they couldn't identify it."

Barron shrugged. "I don't know."

Someone commented, "Looks like you'll need to get tested, Barron." They joked about his young age.

A female coworker, Connie, spoke up. "It's not going to stop with the children. It'll spread. This weapon was just a test. They were testing it, are testing it."

Another person turned to her. "Like test the waters, and if it works, hit us all."

"That's what I think," Connie said.

Barron shook his head. "You have to be one smart scientist to develop a weapon that genetically hits the young and have another on hand to hit everyone else."

"Russians," Lyle Wison said. "Everything they're telling us is a lie. They know something."

"Isn't that obvious?" Connie said.

"But why?" asked Lyle. "That's my big question. Why hit the young first?"

"Compassion," Connie guessed. "Save the kids from the horrors."

John, one of our other cashiers, chuckled. "It's the same argument that people are using for saying it's God's end."

"What do you think, Shel?" Barron asked.

"I think they aren't lying to us. Why would they?" I hung my sweater in my locker. "This is a virus. There's no big story behind it. If it's anything they aren't saying, it's they're not saying how bad it is. Which goes without saying, right? We are under curfew, shopping limitations. That says more than they do. We'll get through this. It'll be over soon."

"Do you really believe that?" Barron asked.

"I have to believe that." I looked down at my watch. "I think I'd go nuts if I believed they were lying and I was trying to figure out the truth."

"A lot of people feel that way," said Barron as he stood and pushed in his chair. "Okay, let's hit the floor and get ready to open. Remember, no arguing. If someone gives you a hard time, say nothing and just put on your lane light. Let the guard handle it."

"The guard didn't help in Philly," Connie added. "A cashier at a Shop and Go was shot."

"Well, you know, that is Philly," Barron stated. "This isn't Philly, this is Hawthorne. We're different."

Were we? We were all the same, just in smaller cities. I was certain our store was going to be as chaotic as the bigger cities.

I put everything else out of my mind, and mentally prepared for manning the register on the floor.

FIVE
Chaotic Moments

I spotted my sons standing in line outside of the grocery store. I could clearly see them on the other side of the window through the newly posted signs about rules of shopping and rations. Four National Guard soldiers paced out on the walk, two were in the store near the front.

One was Gary Applegarth. A young man who worked a bagger at the store when in high school. He was a nice kid, not much older than Sam. But he looked so mature and older.

Did I worry about chaos or problems? No. Maybe a few arguments, but all and all we were a close-knit town.

A close-knit town hit with the tragic loss of so many of our children.

Cal had told me that some people just moved about in a state of shock.

He walked a beat on the street now instead of catching speeders. I worried about him, I did. But he assured me that he was fine.

The mood in the store was a somber one, not much idle talking. Anything that was said was about what was happening, the confusion they had, and, of course, why they could only get one loaf of bread.

We kept the yeast up front as if it were some prized possession or drug. It was something not regulated and people were buying, and sadly, pocketing it.

I never stepped.

Admittedly it was confusing for me at first. What was allowed, items to count, only a few people tried to sneak extra.

There were signs placed throughout the store:

'Take only One.'

'Maximum two per customer.'

We also had a list up front.

Each customer was limited to seven packs of meat, albeit chicken, pork or beef. Barron and his people worked hard now to make sure all packages were a pound or less.

There hadn't been any roasts in weeks.

Nothing big was in the meat department. The deli was pre-sliced and there was a three pound or package limit. The bakery had a sign that fresh buns would return the following week. Canned goods of any type, soup, veggies, pastas were ten per customer. Grains were two. One rice, one pasta. Although another sign stated that the store reserved the right to change quantities based on supply.

I heard the previous week they had run out of boxes of macaroni and cheese and allotted another canned ravioli.

It was crazy. But nothing was so limited that people couldn't make it work.

The first several hours that I was at the register was steady, and after that, while I worked, I watched my sons until they entered the store.

All they had to do was follow the signs, they had enough cash on them,

My hand started aching from ringing groceries in. I stayed in some sort of trance, scanning item after item. No one, even those I knew, said much to me as they bagged their items.

I wished I knew who had lost a child as well, I would have given my condolences, but I barely looked up.

It was like a fine-tuned machine.

In contrast to the horror going on around us, happy music played over the system in the store.

All of it was very strange.

Finally, I saw my sons enter the store, they waved to me and I waved back.

They actually had gotten in my line, but to prevent any problems, Barron moved them to Connie's lane.

They had a full cart and I was proud of them.

Things were going well.

As they left the checkout, I shouted to them to leave a pack of meat out, put the rest in the freezer, and that I would be home soon.

I wanted to kiss them, tell them to be careful, but I couldn't leave my spot.

The shift wasn't overly long—eight hours—but without a break, my legs were hurting, as was my back and there were still a couple hours to go.

Not long after my sons left, the store seemed really crowded, it felt tense.

I was ringing up an order…macaroni, canned ham, rice, bread, tomatoes, counting as I went to ensure people didn't take more than they were allowed.

A part of me didn't care, but then a part of me worried if every one of us eight checkers let one person through with an extra can, and we did that once an hour, that sixty-four cans a day, four hundred and some cans a week.

Looking at it like that kept it in perspective.

I was nearly done with the woman's order; she was helping things move faster by placing her bags in her buggy as I packed them. I could see the person behind her had their driver's license out to show their last name.

I had just rung in a jar of beets when a humming and power down sound happened, just before every light in the store went out.

As if I had to look up to confirm it, I raised my head to the ceiling.

Murmurs began to build, a few seconds later, the voices grew louder.

I didn't know what to do. Surely, the lights would come back on.

"Everyone, keep calm," Barron called out. "The power will be back on in a minute."

Then I saw Gary, the National Guardsman. He was staring outside then rushed over to the other guard. He whispered something to him, then Gary walked over to Barron.

Just as that happened, I noticed outside, traffic had come to a halt. People were stepped out of their cars.

"What's going on outside?" Someone called out.

"Was it an accident?"

"People, please," Barron called out. "Hold your place in line. We'll get you through."

"Hell with this," the woman I was ringing up said. With a sweep of her hand, she knocked her groceries into her cart from the belt and pushed through.

"Hey!" I shouted. "Gary, she didn't pay."

No sooner did that woman decide it was a perfect time to steal a cart of food, others did too.

I could hear Barron pleading, "Mr. Greene, don't do this. Harriet, come on. Stop. People—"

Crash.

The sound of a cart smashing into the automatic doors caught my attention.

Seriously? Not only are you stealing, but now you're breaking out? There aren't enough guards to stop you.

I thought that and then I saw, the woman from my lane was on the ground. Another man was slumped over his cart, his body supported by the handle.

Did they get shot? Did I miss the gunfire?

People started to scream and then the thumping began.

'The Thumping' was the only way I could describe it.

One by one, as if selected, you went down. You stand. You live. You die—people started dropping.

Everywhere.

Gary backed up, holding up his rifle and when the other guardsman next to him dropped, Gary ran.

Connie tried to run and she went down.

Barron held up his hands, his eyes rolled to the back of his head and then he went down too, face first to the ground.

Did he die? Did he pass out?

I wanted to scream, but like Gary all I could do was run.

Was it something in the store? I believed it was and I high-tailed it out of there.

I didn't go back from my sweater or bother to say I was leaving.

People flew from the store with their carts, while some just left empty handed, and like me, once they were outside, they realized it wasn't something happening in the store.

Outside there were screams for help, screams of desperation.

People on the ground, holding their loved ones.

Crying, "Help me. Someone help me."

Didn't they see? There was no one to help.

Maybe I was wrong, but it looked as if half of the people around me were on the ground.

More than anything else, what I witnessed, the loss of power, the dropping of people, I realized we really were under some sort of attack. No natural virus could do what I had just witnessed.

Were we at war and they never told us?

Was my son one of the earliest casualties?

Seeing all that was around me, fear struck.

Sam. Jake. Cal.

Were they like the others, selectively hit? I needed to get home to them.

Moving at a slow pace in my shock, I could feel hands grabbing for me, trying to stop me.

What could I do?

Nothing.

I was desperate, scared, and worried beyond belief for my sons.

Why didn't I kiss them goodbye like I wanted to.

Oh my God, if one of them dropped.

Oh my God.

I couldn't stay there, I couldn't wait, I couldn't help those who cried for it. I had to go. I had to check on my boys.

Once I found them, once I knew they were alright, then we would find Cal.

My children were my priority.

I had already lost one. Please Dear God, don't take another.

With my heart racing, my legs weak, I ran with everything I had, as fast as I could, all the way home.

SIX
CHAOTIC CALM

The short run home felt like miles. My mind raced with every fear imaginable, scared to go home to see. As I turned the bend of my street, I saw our car. It was off to the side of the road, ten houses from our own.

I stopped running. Scared to approach it, every bit of my being trembled. I took a deep breath as I neared it, closed my eyes for a moment, then stepped closer to look inside.

Empty.

I didn't see them near the car, but that didn't mean I could breathe in relief just let. It took Connie a minute or two to fall over.

I didn't see any bodies on the street, not like at the grocery store and around it. There were a few cars and a pickup truck just stopped in the middle of the road, but no bodies.

I picked up my pace again, moving at a fast job.

Neighbors stood outside, talking. It reminded me of the time we were hit with a small microburst, people were out to figure out what had happened.

They looked at me as I passed; I was still wearing my apron from the store, and it was flapping in the wind like some sort of backwards cape.

"Hey, Shel," Mr. Mosely called out my name. "You know what happened here?"

"Huh?"

His question took me by surprise, after all, why would I know? Just because my husband was a police officer in the town didn't mean I was in the loop for everything.

As if I didn't understand him or even the English language, Mr. Mosely slowed down his words and spoke louder. "Do you know what—"

I didn't even bother letting him finish, I ran for my house, calling out, "Sam! Jake!"

Barreling through the door, I yelled for them again.

Our kitchen was at the end of the short hallway and I saw Sam stepped into the doorway.

"Mom? You okay?"

I gasped out, then again, when I saw Jake. I ran to them, hugging them, and I started to cry.

"Mom?" Sam asked. "What happened? What's wrong?"

"I was so afraid you died."

"What?" Sam chuckled. "From a power outage?"

Jake added, "Did you run all the way from the store because of a power outage. That's crazy. We're fine." He backed up. "We had to carry the stuff from the car. We're just trying to figure out what to do with the frozen stuff."

"I think we should put it in the old freezer downstairs," Sam said. "The one we don't use because it's a block of ice."

"Power will be back on soon," Jake commented.

"The car died. What kind of—"

The boys carried on grabbing groceries as if I wasn't speaking at all.

My head spun, were they aloof? I know they saw that I was upset, but they just moved on to other things.

"Stop!" I shouted.

Then my sons looked at me as if I were nuts.

"People are dead," I told them. "Dead. They dropped over. Dead."

I didn't know if they believed me or not, they just stared.

I felt the ability to breathe normally escaped me and I started to hyperventilate.

"Mom, calm down," Sam told me. "Jake, go get Mr. Mosely."

I wanted to say not to get him, but I couldn't catch my breath enough to say so. More panic set in. What was wrong with me?

Mr. Mosely rushed in, telling Jake to get a paper bag, and within a few seconds Jake handed him a paper lunch bag, and Mr. Mosely told me to breathe into it and to sit.

I'm not sure why I didn't think of something so basic myself. Maybe because I was in a state of shock and panic.

"Are you calming down?" Mr. Mosely asked.

Nodding, I started to breathe slower.

"Now, listen to me." Mr. Mosely placed a hand on my shoulder and glanced down seriously at me, speaking again to me like I was a child. "We can't control parts of war; I believe this is part of war. No power, the cars all dying. I believe it is a Nuclear Electro Magnetic Pulse. But it doesn't have to be from a nuclear weapon. A lot of things can cause them."

"Were we hit?" Jake asked. "Wouldn't we see it?"

"Wait." I lowered the bag and waved my hand. "If you know what this is, then why did you ask me if I knew what was happening?"

"I was informing everyone," Mr. Mosely. "Just seeing if you knew."

"Would this weapon have caused people to just drop dead?'

Mr. Mosely shrugged. "If they had a pacemaker."

I stood. "I don't think that many people in Hawthorne had pacemakers."

"What are you talking about?" Mr. Mosely asked.

Sam clarified. "Mom said all kinds of people dropped dead when the power went out."

"Where?" Mr. Mosely asked.

"In town," I answered.

"How many? A few? Dozen?"

"Too many to count."

Slowly, Mr. Mosely stepped back. "Boys, finish putting those groceries away for your mother. I'll be back."

I grabbed his arm as he moved away. "Where are you going?"

"I'm taking a walk to town. I need to see."

"Do you think I'm making it up or imagining it?"

"No," he said. "I just need to see, so I can figure out what is really going on."

I stood. "Then I'm going with you."

"No. you should stay here. You already saw it; you don't need to see it again."

"No, I'm not going to see what happened," I said. "I need to find my husband."

<><><><>

Seventeen years earlier, when Sam was just a baby, we bought our home on Dawson Avenue. We never looked at it as a starter home, because it had enough space for a growing family. At that time, there were only three of us. We had lived in an apartment not far from the Grocery Store and Police Station. Cal had only been on the force for four years at that point.

It was a crummy place, like something straight out of the sixties: green walls, pressed carpet, and paneling everywhere.

We made that house our home, little by little, redoing things until it was just right. Just us.

The first person we met on the street was Mr. Mosely. I still called him that, while Cal moved on to calling him John.

A rugged man, graying hair, in his early fifties. I remembered first meeting Mr. Mosely thinking how fit he was. He was a widower with a grown son, and he had recently retired from the Army, where he had served as a colonel.

He was the first person to show up at our door, and did so the evening of moving day. He brough a tuna noodle casserole and told us how after retiring he discovered his love of cooking. Although, a tuna noodle casserole, in my opinion, wasn't the makings of a culinary masterpiece.

I was wrong. It was delicious.

He helped Cal put our bed together and said that was the most important thing to get done the first day, so we could sleep and be rested to do the remaining work the next day.

He'd moved a lot in his time.

Even though he was crass and sometimes came across as, for lack of a better word, an asshole, I liked him and felt safe around him.

Cal liked him too, but pulled him over all the time for that windshield. I was beginning to think that was a pissing contest between the two of them.

Now, as he and I walked toward town together, that cracked windshield felt an awfully miniscule problem.

As we drew closer to town, Mr. Mosely started asking me what I had seen.

I told him everything I remembered and asked what he thought.

"Let me look and assess," he replied.

I assumed he was going to rely on his years in the military for that assessment.

Just about a block from town, we saw the healthcare and emergency workers carrying people on stretchers.

No ambulances, no sirens.

"The stretchers are a good sign," said Mr. Mosely. "It means people aren't dead. Or at least not all."

"They looked dead."

"Chemical weapons can do that."

I prepared for what we would see. I was too emotional when I ran from there. I still worried about Cal, I hadn't heard or seen him.

When I conveyed my worries to Mr. Mosely, he just calmly told me that my husband was busy.

They had Main Street blocked off when we arrived. Those wooden horse looking things and a couple fireman stood guard.

But there was no questioning or stopping us, they just let us go through. I figured it was because I was Cal's wife, and well, everyone in town knew Mr. Mosely.

It seemed as if every police officer, fireman and paramedic in town was on that street. Helping people, moving people.

Outside of the store, I saw Barron sitting on the sidewalk, a blanket over his shoulders. He looked pale, and held a cloth to his chin while he seemed to be drinking water. He looked so young to me.

Last I saw him he fell to the ground and, saying nothing to Mr. Mosely, I ran to him.

"Barron. You're alright." I gushed then crouched down to him.

"Yeah. Thank God. I need stitches. I didn't break my glasses; that's a good thing." He removed the bloody rag exposing a gaping gash in his chin. "But I'm alive. Glad you are, too."

"The other workers?" I asked.

"I think they're okay. Some were taken to the hospital. They hit their head or something when they fell. But you're okay."

"I'm sorry I ran. I was so worried about my boys."

"I understand." He glanced behind him. "I guess we won't be open for a while."

"It was crazy."

"I know."

"Do you remember anything?" I asked. "Anything at all before you dropped?"

"I just remember being upset because people were stealing. I've passed out once before in my life," he said. "I felt it coming.

But this? Nothing. I was just out of it, but at least it wasn't for long. At least I don't think it was. I woke up on the floor."

"It happened to a lot of people."

"I know. I stumbled out here and saw. Then help just started arriving," he said. "I saw Cal."

I sucked in a breath of shock. "You did? Is he okay?"

"Oh, yeah. Running around here like mad, but he's fine."

"That's why I came back."

"Really?" Barron said in a joking tone. "Not to check on me?"

"No offense, but I thought you died."

"None taken."

"Do you need anything?"

"No. I'm just going to wait for someone to close this hole in my face, then I'm going home and downing my six pack while it's still cold."

"I don't blame you." I stood slowly, turning and looking at the street. "What the hell happened?"

"We're at war."

"That's what everyone's saying, but there was no warning. I watch and read the news. Nothing. I mean, we're a small town. Why would they even hit here?" Then as I looked around, I spotted Todd from the paper. "Speaking of news…"

"Our all-star reporter?"

"Yeah. Maybe he knows something. I'll be back."

Barron wasn't one of my favorite people, but I felt bad leaving him there on the sidewalk. I made a promise to myself that I would go back and check on him, maybe even wait with him until he got help.

Walking to Todd, I spotted Mr. Mosely talking to one of our firemen.

Todd was taking notes and pictures when I approached him.

"Hey, Todd."

"Shel." His eyes cased me, stopping on my apron. "You were working?"

"I was. Yes."

"So, you were here during it all?" Todd asked.

"I was."

"I've been here for fifteen minutes. Were you in the store? I didn't see you."

"No, I ran home."

Todd nodded. "What did you see?'

"The lights went out. People panicked and then they started dropping over."

"Any noises, flashes?"

I shook my head. "No. Not that I saw. It was just pandemonium. But the people dropping didn't go passed this street. At least not to mine."

"You went home?" he asked.

"I did. No one had passed out there. I sounded nuts when I told Mr. Mosely and my boys. Mr. Mosely was the one that came here with me."

"What did Mosely say?"

"That he thinks it's a weapon that causes lights to go out and cars to stop. Sort of like the thing that happens when a nuclear explosion goes off."

"That's a logical explanation."

"Sounds like you think it's something else."

Todd sucked in his lip. "For it to be that it means we're at war, right?"

"Yeah. We were attacked."

"Well—"

"Shel!" Cal called my name. It came from a distance.

I spun around to see my husband running my way.

"Cal," I gushed.

Cal grabbed me and embraced me. "Are you okay?"

"Yes. Shaken up but fine."

"The boys said you were here," Cal said.

"You talked to them? The phones work?" I asked excitedly.

"About the only thing that does," said Cal. "I called to check on you guys. Especially with all this happening."

"Cal," I said softly. "So, they're all okay? Just passed out?"

Todd stepped into our conversation. "I'm curious about that, too."

Cal shook his head. "Not all. We lost about fifteen people so far. Traumatic head wounds and…"

"Pacemakers?" I asked.

Cal widened his eyes. "About four of them, yes. How'd you guess?"

I pointed. "Mr. Mosely."

"Figures. Listen, sweetheart, I have to get back."

"Go. I understand."

Cal darted a kiss to my cheek, then looked at Todd. "Watch her."

"I think she's good," Todd said. "She's with Mosely."

My husband rushed off, back to whatever he was doing. It was hectic and so many people were still on the street waiting for help.

I returned my focus to Todd. "Finish what you were saying."

"About?" Todd asked.

"War. You were acting like you didn't think this was an attack."

Todd waged his fingers. "I didn't say that. I just have my suspicions."

"Okay. I'd love to hear because everything that's been happening around here and this country for the last month is—"

"That's just it," Todd cut me off. "It's not just here. The news isn't saying it. But it's happening everywhere. The kids dying."

"Maybe whoever did this is hitting other places."

"Like Russia?" Todd asked.

"Yes. Or somewhere else."

"Only a few countries have the ability to develop a sophisticated weapon and deliver it at this magnitude, and I spoke to my friend in DC. There's not a single place immune to this."

"What?" I stumbled back a little in shock. "No."

"Yes." Todd nodded. "It's global. If we're at war, who is the enemy. And if we're not at war," he said, "then what the hell is going on?"

SEVEN
Searching for Answers

After returning home, my mind was still reeling from things Todd told me. Despite everything Mosely said to reassure me, I did what any good Catholic girl would do: I went home and dug out that big, red, hardback bible that belonged to my mother.

It was used more for pressed flowers and funeral home prayer cards nowadays than for prayer and reflection.

Cal, who was Presbyterian, always pointed out that I never read it while we'd been together.

It was okay.

I knew about the book of Revelation. The funny thing—maybe it wasn't funny—but the bible I had was so old, that it wasn't called Revelation, it was called Apocalypse. And that was what I felt we were facing. Pure biblical, end of the world stuff.

Bring on the disasters.

In my living room, using candlelight, a flashlight, and magnifying glass, I read that last book of the bible over and over. I tried with diligence to find sections that coincided with what was going on. Surely, in my mind, this wasn't war.

This was God.

I didn't tell that to Mr. Mosely because I was certain he would say something along the lines of '*Oh, nutcracker, it is.*'

But just like I didn't have enough to prove that it was divine destruction, Mr. Mosely and Cal didn't have enough to say it wasn't.

As I was reading Apocalypse for umpteenth time, Cal walked into the room. I'd heard him come in earlier, but I had no concept of how long ago that was. Cal wasn't sleeping much; he had to be on shift, keeping people calm, watching the stores.

"I'm off," he said. "Make sure the boys don't open the freezer downstairs. It's such a block of ice, we're good for a while."

"What time is it?" I asked.

"Five."

"I'm sorry, I didn't go to bed."

"You're…" He sat down. "Researching."

"I am." I gave him a gentle smile. "How are you?"

"I'm okay. You?"

"Not as bad as I could be. A part of me isn't scared, because if all this is right," I lay my hand on the bible. "I'll see Luke again."

"Shel, there's an explanation for all of this. We just don't know it yet." Cal leaned into me and kissed my forehead. "If I hear anything, I'll let you know."

"Thank you."

Cal grunted as he stood from the couch.

"Doesn't matter though, does it?" I asked.

He paused. "What do you mean?"

"We can't control what is going on. Whether it's God's will, or that of a foreign country end, or nature. Any way you look at it, whatever the cause, this is the end."

Knowing my husband as well as I did, I knew the look he gave me said it all. A glance of agreement that what I said was true.

We were just normal people, and no way to prove our theories or thoughts. With no power, no news, there was no way to find out anything. We were in the dark, all the way around.

After Cal had left, I extinguished the candle, not realizing how much of it I used.

I wasn't sure how many more we had, and batteries certainly were in short supply in our house.

I caught a couple hours of sleep on the couch. When I woke, I checked on the boys; they were still asleep. After leaving a note on the fridge, telling them I'd be back soon, I ventured out.

There were a couple places I wanted to go. The store was one of them. Having worked there for as long as I did, I felt an obligation.

Did they need my help in organizing things, or cleaning up?

Rescues crews were still on the street, although no victims were there. They were there mainly for clean-up and moving cars. The store was closed and a guard was out front.

"I don't think they're going to open today," said the guard.

"I figured as much," I replied. "I work here. I was coming to see if they needed help getting things back together. It went a little nuts yesterday."

"I can see." He pointed to the windows.

I peeked inside, some carts full of groceries remains, check-out lines still had food on the belts.

"Everything," he said, "is nuts."

"I know. You're not from around here, are you?"

"No Ma'am, Cleveland."

"Have you spoken to your mother to let her know you're alright."

"I have."

"Good."

"I did receive word that the manager planned on coming in at zero nine hundred hours."

I glanced at my watch. "Thank you for that."

With that in mind, and not wanting to stand outside in awkward silence or idle conversation for an hour with the guard, I made my way to my other destination.

The church.

Somehow, in my mind, I thought it was a novel idea. I'd go in, a few candles would be lit, and some priest would see me and talk to me.

He would have religious insight.

What I saw when I went into the church was not what I envisioned in my mind.

It was packed.

Quiet, yet crowded. Every pew had people in it. Some kneeling, some sitting. Some people were at the altar lighting candles, while others must have spent the night. They were sound asleep in the back of the church.

I wanted to go in, find a seat, wait for some miraculous answer to come, but I changed my mind.

If people were sleeping there, they didn't have answers.

Like me they flocked to what they believed was a sanctuary. But that church was no safer than the street or my house.

I felt silly, like a fraud for going there when I rarely ever did.

I decided to just walk back home and head down to the store in a little bit.

There was a different feel to everything. A quietness that engulfed the air, a sadness that was undeniable.

We all lost, and we all felt it.

The walk did me some good, but I could use a cup of coffee. I hadn't figured out how to make that yet without electricity.

It was still early when I returned to my street. First thing I saw, and I hadn't noticed it when I ran home the previous day, was an empty grocery store cart in the yard at the corner house.

The Dearling Home.

I don't know why, but it angered me. If they had the cart, they'd run off and not paid. Then I took a second to be rational. Maybe she paid for her stuff and her car wouldn't start. I tried telling myself that, giving them the benefit of the doubt.

A few more houses close to my own was when I heard it.

It sounded like a radio broadcast, someone talking about Spain and the loss of power there.

A radio?

Who had a radio playing.

I should have known who it was, because the sound came from Mr. Mosely's home.

Drawing closer, his garage was open and clearly the radio came from there. I saw him walk around his old car; the hood was up.

I walked up his driveway.

"Morning," I called out.

He stepped back from the hood of his car. "Morning, Shel." He walked to his work bench and lifted a mug. To his right was an old tin percolator and I watched as he poured coffee. "Did you want some?"

"I would love some."

"Hold on." He walked through the garage door, which I knew led into his kitchen and returned a minute later with a cup. He poured me some and handed it to me. "Can't guarantee how good it is. I had to pull out this old thing. It was Cindy's when we first got married. She got it from her grandmother. I made it on the grill."

I took a sip of the warm brew. It was wonderful. "Thank you so much."

"You're welcome." He gulped another drink, set down his mug and lifted his tool. "What brings you here?'

"I went to the store."

He paused before returning to under his hood. "They aren't open."

"Clearly. I wanted to see if I could help get things back together. It would keep my mind off of things. I'll head back down in a little bit."

"Good idea." He disappeared under the hood.

"Then I went to the church."

He poked his head from the side and looked at me. "The church."

"For answers."

"To?"

"What's going on."

"Church doesn't have the answers. I'm a man of faith myself, but…" He grunted, doing something under that hood. "This isn't a God thing."

"A man thing."

"Maybe. Maybe not. Who knows?"

"I heard the radio," I said. "That's why I came to your garage. Not that the coffee isn't a bonus."

"There's nothing really new, if you wanna know."

"I don't know what's happening."

"No one does. I have it on in case there's an emergency message from the government or a breakthrough. But it's not the news. It's people saying what they see and hear."

"Are you learning anything?" I asked.

"Some. Not much more than we know."

"How do you have a radio?" I asked.

"Oh." He closed the hood to his car and walked around. "It's an old receiver. I hooked it up to a battery and got it to work. I can't send a message, but I can hear. I promise to let you know if I hear anything."

"Is that your polite way to tell me to go away."

Mr. Mosely laughed. "No. I was just telling you that." He opened his car door. "Now, fingers crossed."

"Okay. Why?"

"Because I am hoping she starts."

"All cars died yesterday," I said.

"They did. And if it is what I think it was that caused it, then something I learned in the Army when they trained us. Change the Solenoid."

"And you just had one hanging about."

"I'd like to say 'doesn't everyone,' but they don't. I knew that this car was old and I wanted to have spare parts." He slid into the driver's seat and cranked the car.

It started.

"Ha, ha!" he cheered, then immediately shut it off. "It works."

"You're so resourceful. Radio to a battery, an extra car part, and coffee on a grill." I took a sip and held up my cup.

"Well, I wouldn't say coffee on a grill is resourceful," he said.

"I would. I wouldn't have thought about it."

"I'm gonna tell you a secret Shel: pretty soon, you'll be resourceful."

"Why is that?" I asked.

"You'll adapt and learn," he said. "Take the knowledge from the technology that you are used to and make things work."

"You don't think things will get back to normal."

Mr. Mosely walked to the front of his car and shut the hood. "No, I don't."

"But they have to, right? I mean, the president has to be doing something."

"Have you heard from him? I haven't. I've been listening to radio chatter for twelve hours. No one has mentioned him."

I gasped. "You don't think he's dead, do you?"

"Nope." Mr. Mosely returned to his coffee mug. "I think he's tucked neat and safe in a bunker somewhere."

"If the virus is only hitting kids, why is he in a bunker?"

Mr. Mosely just glanced at me.

"Do you think there's going to be a nuclear war? Oh my God."

He lifted his hand to stop me. "I don't know. But I *do* know this: we are at war. They can say it's mother nature, but this all has the makings of a prelude to a ground invasion. People are resources, without them you can't rebuild. People are also fighters. They'll fight. We as humans are territorial."

"But they're saying the virus is everywhere."

Mr. Mosely nodded. "They are. But who is to say, it just didn't get ahead of whatever country did this and they are experiencing it too? They're invading, but it won't happen yet. First, they take out as many people as they can before resorting to attacks and destruction. Then that's the next step. After that, they start picking people off. The biggest thing that is screwed up is they hit the kids. Damn shame."

A lump formed in my throat and it took all that I had to swallow it.

"I'm sorry, Shel, that was insensitive."

"No, it's okay." I shook my head.

"Do me a favor, Shel, don't tell anyone. I mean anyone that I have a working car. Not even your husband."

I tilted my head and looked at him curiously. "Okay, but…why?"

"I have a working car. No one else does. Someone finds out, they may try to get it. Make a run for it. I would. I *am*."

"Making a run for it?" I asked.

"When the time is right."

"Do you really think someone around here would steal your car. This is Hawthorne, these are our neighbors."

"Desperate times brings out desperate actions. If you asked me last week if Mrs. Dearling would be stealing food, I'd scoff. Yet, yesterday, there she was running up the street with a buggy full of unbagged groceries."

"I knew it."

"Yep." Mr. Mosely nodded.

"I'll keep your secret. I promise only if you do one thing for me."

"What's that?" he asked.

"Before the time is right, before you know you have to leave, can you teach me and my boys some of these survival things."

"Absolutely."

"Thank you." I walked to the work bench to set down my mug. "And thank you for the coffee."

"Keep the cup." He poured more coffee into it. "Send your boys over when you head back to the store. I'll start talking to them."

I gave him a smile of thanks and told him I'd let him get back to what he was doing. I left with that warm and wonderful coffee clutched between both my hands.

There was a part of me that knew, I may be that old dog that couldn't learn new tricks, but my boys were young enough. I saw what I believed was the tip of the iceberg in what Mr. Mosely knew and what he could do.

If my boys learned just a little, I would be happy.

Whatever was coming our way, I wanted my boys to survive. It didn't matter if I did or Cal, but they had to. I truly believed Mr. Mosely had not only knowledge to share, but insight on using instincts that was invaluable, and worth keeping the car secret from my husband.

EIGHT
Passing Time to Normalcy

Four days.

Four days of darkness and silence.

I still held hope that everything would eventually return to normal, but how could it?

The children of our town were gone, at least half of them.

Cal was exhausted, he had been working non-stop since the lights went out. My kids were spending more time with Mr. Mosley than their own father.

I helped out at the store, putting things back in order, but more importantly doing inventory.

No shipments arrived, nor did Barron expect any to.

Usually when a major event occurred, there was no break from the news about it. When the Youngen Virus, as people called it, was in full swing, there was no break at all from the news.

Then it stopped

The lights went out and we were clueless as to who was behind it all. My sources of information, Mr. Mosley and Todd had nothing new to offer. The guardsmen offered a speck of intel, but even they had no word as to when the rationing would continue.

Barron wanted to meet at the store to discuss an idea he had.

I gave Mr. Mosley some ground beef in exchange for looking after and feeding my boys, and I made my way to the store.

Surprisingly, on my walk there, Cal was out front of the Dearling home.

"Where are you headed?" he asked.

"The store. Barron wants us to come in. He has an idea."

"About?"

"Considering it's a grocery store, I'm gonna say food."

"Okay well, once the guard pulls out, I want you nowhere near there."

"Is the guard pulling out?" I asked.

"They will eventually. And people are stealing now."

"In Hawthorn?"

"Yeah. Dearling lost a lot of their last ration order."

I chuckled, a smirk spreading across my face.

"What?" Cal asked.

"They stole it, so what goes around comes around."

"Shel, come on."

"Just saying and I'm gonna head down there. Boys are with Mr. Mosley."

"Again?"

"He's teaching them survival things. It's better than them just sitting at home."

"I guess."

"I'll wait up for you. Let's try to make time tonight."

"Sounds like a plan." Cal gave me a quick kiss goodbye, and I was on my way.

Everything felt unfinished, unresolved. I hated that I'd lost my son but I was glad it was in the beginning. At least we got a proper goodbye. So many families didn't have that chance; they couldn't even grieve properly.

I arrived at the grocery store; I was the only employee there other than Barron.

Our guardsman was drinking a can of soda and held the door for me.

"So, I was doing a quick inventory," Barron said.

"We're not open, and we counted yesterday," I said.

"Yes, but when I walked in, the cereal and canned goods looked scarce. One can of spam left."

"Had to be employees," I said. "I mean the guard is letting us in. It has to be."

"I was thinking that."

"Especially since no one but me showed up tonight to talk about this. So, what's the plan?"

"I was going to suggest, if things are back to normal or we know what to do with this, then maybe we pass it out. First to families that need it then other but…" he just stopped talking.

"But?"

"I honestly believe in a few days people are gonna find their way in here, it will be looted."

"You really think that?" I asked.

"I do. Don't you?"

"I'm so sadly disappointed in this town. I thought we were close. People are stealing. People we know. And pretty soon nothing will be safe."

"I agree. So, what do we do?"

"They want to loot, let's make it look like it's been looted. Leave a few things out ready," I said. "Padlock it until we know it's needed."

"I like that idea. How long do you think it will take us to do it?" Barron asked.

"We can start now. I'm here; you got me."

"Thank you, I appreciate it," Barron said. "I thought I'd be the only one."

"Well, your grandfather would be proud of your dedication."

Barron grumbled softly. I knew that was a habit. He loved and adored his grandfather, but being the manager at his family grocery store wasn't on his priority list. From what I learned, Barron had a shot at a career in science and technology. He had just graduated from MIT, and was supposed to return in the fall to their graduate program, when his grandfather passed away.

His grandfather was the owner and manager when I first started working there. I knew that his grandfather raised Barron when his parents were killed in an airplane crash.

I don't remember that happening, but I knew he was young when he lost them. The crash was caused by faulty technology, and some round town always said that was why Barron dove nose first into the subject.

But his prospects and intelligence didn't stop his grandfather from making him work. Barron worked in the store throughout high school, and sometimes when he was on break from college. Never did any of us expect Barron to step into his grandfather's shoes.

He claimed it was short term, but that was two years ago.

Now, the man who was voted most likely to create an invention to change the future, was changing prices and organizing rations when he should have been changing the world and attending frat parties.

"Let's count first." Barron handed me the clipboard and he grabbed a buggy. We began with aisle one.

He counted them as he put them in the cart, leaving one or two on the shelves here and there.

Aisle one. Salad dressings, condiments.

"Eight," Barron said of the ketchup.

I marked it down. "When's the last time you were out of Hawthorne?"

"That's a strange question."

"Just curious."

"Before the Youngen Virus, for sure," Barron answered. "Two mustard."

"Strange we had nine. Who steals mustard?" I shrugged and jotted down.

"You?"

"Me? Why would I steal mustard?"

"No." Barron chuckled. "You asked me, I'm asking you. When's the last time you were out of Hawthorne? Four relishes."

"No one is taking relish? I would think that's more sustainable than mustard." I wrote the number. "It was before we lost Luke. Do you know anyone that's been out of Hawthorne since this all started?"

Barron shook his head. He extended his hand to the steak sauce and stopped. "Why?"

"Because we're shut off. No power, no news, no cars. No means to leave. Sometimes I wonder if we're the only ones affected, and they're keeping us locked up. I know it's crazy, like some sort of government conspiracy where we're all left to die, but I can't help but wonder."

"That's crazy, not in an insane way, but…" Barron counted items. "Here's something even crazier. Two sweet pickles, four black olives."

"I'm confused. How is that crazy?"

"Jot the inventory down." He pointed.

I did.

"The sweet pickles and black olives aren't crazy. When I called your thought about being the only ones affected crazy, I mean it was crazy because I had a similar thought."

"No way. What is it?"

Barron paused. "That because we're such a small town, the only reason we are cut off is because we are the only ones left."

"What about the radio stuff that Mr. Mosely and Todd picked up."

"Small town survivors like us," Barron said.

"Whoa."

"What?"

"That's a great theory."

Barron nodded. "Sadly, we'll never know unless we find someone that has been out there. Let's finish this. At this rate it will be supper by the time we're done."

We continued on, aisle by aisle.

After another complete inventory, which showed how much was actually missing, we set to task making the store look like a movie set to some end of the world story. Empty shelves, cans toppled. The meat section had been barren for days before the blackout. The only thing we couldn't really do much about was the miniscule amount of produce. Most of that would be bad within days.

After we both took a sack of apples and potatoes for ourselves, we loaded the remainder of the produce into grocery carts with plans to hit Factory Three.

Factory Three was on the edge of Hawthorne, covering three streets, with low-cost houses. It was where a lot of the people who lost their jobs when the shoe factory closed down fifteen years earlier had ended up.

Barron commented that he hadn't seen many of them in the store lately, and he knew everything that came in.

It wouldn't take long; we'd drop off the produce—some cereal and canned goods—then I'd head home.

I was proud of all we accomplished, though I didn't realize how late it was until the store started getting dark. I heard Sam's voice echo in the store as he called out.

"Mom? Are you okay?"

I pushed my cart toward the front of the store where Sam stood with Jake.

"Hey." I was surprised to see them. "What are you doing here?"

"Mr. Mosely sent us," Sam replied. "He said you were gone too long and was worried."

"Well, that was nice of him."

"What happened here?" Jake asked. "When was it looted?'

I turned around and gave Barron a high five.

"What?" Sam asked confused.

"We made it look this way," I replied.

"Why?" questioned Jake.

"Because people were stealing," I answered. "If they think the store was already looted, there's nothing else to steal."

"Where's the food?" Sam asked.

"Locked up and secure. Except for this." I indicated to my cart. "We're headed to Factory Three."

"You boys are welcome to join us," Barron said. "We have four carts."

Jake and Sam looked at each other, shrugged with a 'why not look' and we all headed there together.

The wheels of the carts squeaked as we pushed them down the main street. It was empty and quiet, and as the sun set, we were the only ones out there.

We passed a few guardsmen on the way, no one said anything.

I had been to the Factory Three neighborhood four times in my entire life. It seemed each time was seven years apart. And each time the houses grew more dilapidated.

Three streets, no more than a block each. A section of housing removed from the rest of the town, as if it were the red-headed stepchild of Hawthorne.

The backdrop of the housing section was the closed factory, dark and ominous. Between the houses and factory was an overgrown parking lot and a field.

There were a few trailers, row houses, all rental properties.

Horror stories were told about landlords from out of state, that were nothing more than *slum* lords. While the properties were cheap, they weren't maintained to code standards.

It wasn't always like that though. The first time I was there was when I was a teenager and a friend of mine lived in one of the row houses. Back then it was nice. It was affordable before the factory closed, and a short walk to work. The people who lived there now were poor. I supposed every town had an area like that.

If anyone was to get the food, they were the best ones to get it.

There was a gas station on the corner just before Factory Three.

That, of course, was closed down since the power went out. The windows were boarded up and a handwritten sign on the pumps read, 'No power no gas'.

We knew there were three streets and four carts, we each had a grocery cart packed with bags of produce and food. The plan was to drop a bag at each house randomly and quietly, they'd find them in the morning, and if there were any bags left, we would take them to the Senior Living Center, four blocks away.

Sure, it was a lot to do, but all we had was time.

It was on the cusp of nightfall as we turned the bend to enter Factory Three, and I knew right away something was wrong.

It was dark.

Darker than normal. No signs of candlelight or people, nothing.

At least on our street people were outside until it was time to go to bed. Either staring up at the sky, talking with neighbors or cooking on a grill.

But there was none of that.

"Did everyone leave?" Sam asked. "Why is it so quiet?'

"I don't know."

Barron lifted a bag of groceries and walked to the first house. He knocked on the door.

Nothing.

He knocked again, then turned around. "I don't think anyone is here."

Inspired by his bravery to just walk up to a stranger's house and knock, I did the same at the next home.

I realized by the fourth house, we could knock all night.

No one would answer.

Plain and simple.

Factory Three was empty and everyone that lived there was gone.

NINE
THE FACTORY IS CLOSED

When I told Mr. Mosely about Factory Three, his attitude conveyed that it was nonsense. He didn't believe it.

He used one of his famous scoffing lines, "Oh, nuts in a sock, they're there, they are hiding." Then as if to prove a point, he went off and checked.

Forty minutes later he came back and said, "They're gone. No one is there."

"Are they dead?" Jake asked.

"Jake," I scolded.

"Don't snap at the boy for being realistic," said Mr. Mosely. "I thought the same thing. Maybe they're dead. A gas leak, or something. But I kinda…sort of…went into one of the homes. One that looked as if someone still lived there. Car in the driveway, bike in the yard. Garbage cans full. So, I went to the back door. It was unlocked."

"And?" I asked.

"Not there. House was empty. And the strangest thing? They left food, clothes…pictures," he said. "It was like they just disappeared."

Immediately upon hearing that, I went into murder-mystery mode. Like I was some sort of detective and there was more to the story.

What happened to the people in Factory Three?

I waited for a little while for Cal to get home, then Sam, Jake, and I took a walk back to Factory Three. I wanted to count the houses, estimate how many people were there. Moreso, stand in the street and yell out.

Which we did.

Nothing. No response. A confirmation of Mr. Mosely's assessment that everyone was gone. Or at least it appeared that way.

Sam went back home and Jake stayed with me.

Everything was another aspect, adding to the one big giant mystery building around us.

I hated that the power went out, and that the news was gone. Was something going on outside of Hawthorne and we were locked down, or was Barron right and the world ended around us?

Our town wasn't that big and I knew my husband was making rounds, checking on things.

The weather was nice, it wasn't cold or hot, and Jake and I walked the streets.

Was Factory Three the only section of town mysteriously gone?

We made our way to the newspaper building, hoping to find Todd. I didn't know where he lived, and the office was closed. We left a note for him to contact us.

On our way back home, Cal found us.

"Shel? Jake?" Our names were called through the darkness.

We were at the end of Main Street, just about to head toward home when we saw Cal.

"You guys know there's a curfew, right?" Cal asked as he approached us. "What are you doing out?"

"Is it that late?" I asked.

"Yeah, what are you guys doing out?"

"Factory Three," I replied. "When is the last time you patrolled there or walked a beat?"

"I don't know, Shel, same as every neighborhood. There's only seven of us left. Two or three days."

"Two or three days since you were there?"

"Yeah." He nodded.

"Was everything okay?"

"As okay as anyone could be. Why?"

"They're gone," I said.

"Who?"

"Factory Three."

"Alright, again, I'll repeat. Who at Factory Three is gone?"

"Everyone," I told him. "Every man, woman, child, animal. Gone. It's a ghost town."

Like with Mr. Mosely, Cal looked at me in utter disbelief. There was no reason for me to stand there and argue or try to convince him. Like with Mosely, he would have to see for himself.

Cal left to do that.

When he returned, he was baffled and confirmed what I had told him.

Three blocks of Hawthorne residents were done. No explanation, no clue as to where they went, they just disappeared, and I had a feeling, it was going to be a long time, if at all, when we found out what happened to them all.

TEN

FAMILY TIME AND COMPANY

It took longer than I had hoped, but I finally got my wish.

My family spending the evening together.

Cal finally had an evening off, and even though things around us were far from normal, it felt good to be together.

I think I was the only just waiting for things to be the way they were. I knew they wouldn't be the same after all the death. But I believed, possibly naively, that we'd move on and the power would return.

After all, someone out there had to be working on the problem. People don't just drop dead and the lights go out without authorities trying to make things right.

It was just a matter of time.

Maybe I wasn't fully understanding, or maybe it was wishful thinking. Until the day came when we'd be back in our normal stride, I was going to enjoy the moments like I had with my family in the living room over a late supper.

"Thirteen days," Cal said as he swiped on spoon through a bowl of Mr. Moseley chili. "That's how long it took."

"Thirteen days?"

Cal nodded then looked at the boys. "I counted; it was thir-teen days for the virus to wipe out the world in *The Stand*."

"Wow," I said. "I can't believe you know that."

Sam Chuckled. "I can't believe Dad went back and counted."

Jake added. "As if Stephen King is a psychic."

Cal shrugged. "Maybe."

Jake shook his head. "Virus stopped. Ever think maybe it's not another country doing this."

I waved out my hand. "I went down that God-road."

"No," Jake said. "Not God. Or even Mother Nature for that matter."

"Then who's left?" I asked.

Sam answered. "I think he thinks it's aliens"

"And don't laugh," said Jake. "Mr. Mosley didn't. He said nothing can be ruled out."

"Jake." Cal reached over and patted him on the knee. "I won't laugh but I don't think it's a species from outer space."

"Then what?" Jake asked. "If every country was hit by the Youngen virus, who did it? They didn't do it to themselves."

"Not on purpose," Cal said. "More than that it could have been an accidental release of a biology agent and no one wants to take the blame."

"It's very specific," Jake said. "Calculated."

"Can we not talk about this over dinner?" I said. "It's the first time in weeks we've been together as a family and I'd like to talk about anything else."

"Mom," Sam called me. "What is there to talk about but this? There's no television or sports, we didn't have school unless you count hanging out with Mr. Mosley, but isn't that like talking about it?"

"Not really." Jake shrugged. "We learned that cool thing today."

"What is that?" I asked.

Jake explained, "How to open a can without a can opener. All the cans for the chili were opened without one."

"Doesn't he have one?" I asked.

"He does," Jake replied. "But he was showing us how in case we don't have one. There are three ways actually."

"Next time we have to open a can," I said. "You can show me."

"Is there anything," Cal asked, "we can talk about that doesn't relate somehow to this situation?"

Before anyone could respond, a knock came at the door. I looked over my shoulder to see Mr. Mosley standing on the other side of the screen porch door.

I strode from the floor. "He probably needs his pot back." I walked to the door waving for him. To come in as I did.

Mr. Mosley stepped inside. "Sorry to interrupt."

Cal stood as well. "Not a problem. Please come in. The chili was excellent."

"Thank you but I'm not here for my pot." He lifted his eyebrow and looked at me. "You folks may want to think about packing your stuff up." He shifted his eyes looking at each of us. "We have a problem."

Pack up. Go south. Toward the hills of Kentucky.

This is what Mr. Mosley told us, and it angered me. It took everything I had not to say, "that's easy for you to suggest you have a car."

But I didn't.

I bit my tongue, keeping my promise.

Todd was gone, and that screamed a warning to Mr. Mosley. Although I wasn't quite sure how he knew Todd had left, or how he got out. I wondered that for myself too.

"He must have figured out how to get a car running," Mr. Mosley said. "At least George Smithton's classic."

"The solenoid," Cal said. "I heard the guard talking about trying to replace electrical parts."

"That's what I think," said Mr. Mosley. "If Todd, the golden boy, took off then one of his sources gave him intel."

"Do you know what it could be?" I asked. "I mean you have to have an inkling if you're telling us to pack up and walk twenty miles to the woods."

"There's chatter." Mr. Mosley placed his hands on his hips. "It doesn't make sense how, but if it's true then we have got to get further away. We are too close to Cincinnati."

Again, there I was thinking how easy it would be for him to get in his car and go. But what about us?

"What kind of chatter?" Cal asked.

"One of the guardsmen confirmed that he heard the same," Mr. Mosley said. "There's talk that we've lost control of our instruments."

I didn't know what that meant, and stared at him with a puzzled look.

Cal sought clarification. "Instruments? Meaning?"

"Military instruments. Missile defense, launching. More importantly, it looks like NORAD is reporting the system in compromised," Mr. Mosely said. "One man on the radio said that one of the operators there claimed someone else was running the controls."

Cal chuckled. "That doesn't make sense. We all know, through the years, NORAD has been anything but flawless."

"True," Mr. Mosely said. "But here's the deal, they always reported false alarms. Like strikes that weren't coming. We know for a fact that something came through without being detected. If this Youngen Virus was a weapon, they missed it. What else have they missed?"

Cal exhaled heavily, swiped his hand down his face and paced backwards. "What? So, I just leave my post, pack up my family and go, wait, walk where? How do we take the supplies? Luke's old red wagon? A grocery cart? Where do we go?"

"Take Old Hathaway Road, stay near the trees until you get farther south or east. We need to get to Florence, or even Louisville. I have a list of shelters."

Sam excitedly asked, "How? How did you get them?"

"I had them," said Mr. Mosely. "I've been reaching out."

"Florence," said Cal. "That's doable. That's about twelve miles. But if we're already too close to Cincinnati, what is twelve miles going to do?" My husband lifted his hand. "I'm not doubting your expertise…"

"Not thinking that you are. I'm just giving my two cents."

"Let me think about it," Cal said. "The Mayor has a town meeting planned day after tomorrow, I think we should be there to hear what he says. It's been quiet. Nothing has been happening lately."

Air airy chuckle escaped me without me thinking about it and Cal shot a glance my way.

"What was that?" he asked.

"Nothing has been happening. An entire part of town vanished."

"They didn't vanish," Cal scolded.

"They vanished. Gone. They took nothing."

"You don't know that," Cal stated.

"You went there yesterday. What did you see?" I asked.

"They left. Maybe even evacuated like Mr. Mosely wants to do. Factory Three didn't just vanish."

"What if they did?" Jake asked. "I mean seriously, what if they did?"

Cal turned with a wave of his hand. "This isn't a sci-fi novel or movie. They didn't just vanish. It doesn't happen."

Jake shook his head. "What about the crew of the *Mary Celeste*? In 1872 they vanished and left all supplies behind. Roanoke, that colony, the people gone."

Sam nodded. "Atlantis."

Silence.

"Okay." Cal lifted his hand in surrender. "If they vanished, what happened? Huh?"

"To Atlantis?" Sam asked. "Oh, I don't know, that's still a big mystery."

Cal cringed. "I'm not talking about Atlantis; I'm asking Jake, since he is hell bent on saying that they vanished. I'm curious to know how."

Jake's mouth opened to reply.

"And don't say aliens," Cal warned.

Jake shut up.

"In his defense," Sam said. "He's fifteen."

"And?" Cal asked.

"He's fifteen," Sam repeated. "He doesn't have the knowledge we have."

"And on that." Mr. Mosely gave a single clap to his hands. "I'm out of here. I'll give it to the mayor's town meeting, to see if he has anything to say, after that, I'm leaving. I'm hitting a shelter. In my opinion we were attacked and it's not the end."

I looked at Mr. Mosely as he headed to the door. "How?"

"Excuse me?"

"How are you going to go?" I asked.

"Any means necessary." He stared at me as if to convey that he knew I was calling him out on his car. Then he left.

I stood there, staring at the door in disbelief. I really wanted to turn around and blast out that he had a working car.

Break that promise.

It bothered me. He was all about running to the hills but didn't mention how he was going to do that when he obviously did know how.

Then again, I was assuming he was going to go by himself. Maybe he came over because he was going to throw us in his old Dodge.

"Well, that was an interesting turn of the night," Cal said. "Shel?"

I stepped back from the door, then closed it, still staring. "Yeah, it was."

"Alright, can we go back to just sitting together?" Cal asked. "Being a family and following Mom's rule about not talking about this."

Sam asked, "Do you think we'll evacuate? Should we start getting things ready?"

"No," Cal replied. "It's craziness. Someone has control of the military controls. All from radio chatter. No. We go nowhere unless I think we should. That's my decision."

Slowly, arms folded tight to my body. I turned around. "Cal, I love you."

"I love you, too."

"But the who the hell are you to make the final call if this family evacuates or not?"

Cal looked shocked. "What?"

"You heard me," I stated calmly. "You're out there every day, checking on things. Are they normal? People are stealing, looting, we don't have power. People are dead. Children are dead. It's not a power company thing. The cars don't work. It can only be an attack."

"That's not true," Cal argued. "Science tells us that the same thing happened in 1859. We learned about this is high school."

"The Carrington Event?" I asked.

"Yes."

"That lasted two days, Cal. Two days. We've gone four, and Carrington didn't have half the kids under the age of thirteen just die. This is more, this is bigger. I think it's an attack. I feel it. So, before you make your final decision on the fate of me and my children, open your mind to what could be happening."

"And what is that?" Cal asked.

"I don't know, but it's not good and it's not normal!"

"And I'm supposed to just pack up my family and head to the hills on that?"

"No." I shook my head. "*We*…we are supposed to pack up our family, because we don't know what's next."

I couldn't remember the last time Cal and I even argued, yet there we stood, staring each other down.

After a minute, my oldest broke the tension.

"Is family time over?" Sam asked. "If not, can I make a suggestion? We know what we're going to do if we don't leave, how about we talk as a family about what we will do it we do leave?"

It was a great idea, one that Cal didn't embrace, but for the sake of the boys, he went along with it.

I loved my husband to death, but he had to know, if I knew leaving was the only way to keep my sons safe, with or without him, we were going.

In a way that made me as guilty as him for single handedly deciding the fate of our family.

Clearly, only one of us was right, but which one remained unknown for now.

ELEVEN
WHO'S MINDING THE STORE?

"I'm sorry."

Mr. Mosely was only trying to help. When I saw him, I knew I should apologize.

"What for?" he asked.

"When you were at the house, I asked how you were going to leave."

"Ah. Okay. Yes." He nodded.

"I didn't say anything. I promised," I told him.

"Really?" he asked.

"Really. It's your business and it was something I learned. I don't know why I acted like that."

"It's fine. I couldn't come out and say I was going to drive your family," he said.

"Are you?" I asked.

"Of course. I've taught your boys quite a bit rather fast," he said. "But we aren't moving very fast in the car."

"Is it broken?"

"No. We need more supplies than the car can handle, so it will be a slow move when we go."

I lowered my head.

"What's wrong?"

"Cal. He doesn't see a reason to leave. It's been an argument between us."

"He'll see. Don't you worry," Mr. Mosely said. "Tomorrow is the mayor's meeting. I have hopes that he's going to say something we don't know."

"Do you really believe that?"

After a pause, he shook his head. "No. But I have a gut feeling that the meeting tomorrow morning is going to change everything."

"I'll leave without him if I have to. I want to protect my sons. I've already lost one."

"It won't come to that."

"Have you given any thought to Factory Three?" I asked.

"I have. And I don't know. I don't know what happened to those folks. It just seems strange to me that the portion of town that no one really paid much attention to is gone. All of them. Not a handful, but all. How is that possible?"

"Sacrifice."

"What?" Mr. Mosely laughed at his question.

"Maybe sacrifice is a strong word, but it's like they were given up for a cause."

"I'm gonna just say that's sort of a far-fetched idea. Who would sacrifice a part of a small town? We're nothing. We're a nothing town. Those folks left for a reason and they just didn't tell anyone."

"What if we're not a nothing town?" I asked. "What of something big happened here or there's a secret?"

"Again, I'm gonna disagree. Hawthorne is a dot on the map in the foothills of Kentucky. Nothing ever happened here and nothing ever will. But you keep working on it."

Dismissed.

I felt as unheard as my son Jake when he spewed forth his alien theories.

I asked Sam what he thought and he just didn't know.

There was only one person in town he seemed to think as outlandishly as me and Jake, and that was Barron.

The phones still worked and I tried to call him; no answer.

After talking with Mr. Mosely, I walked down to the store.

Apparently, Barron had been there since he and I were last in the store. The windows were boarded up and the guard was gone. I left a note on the back employee door for him, and then I walked over to Factory Three.

A ghost town.

Even in the daylight it looked spooky. It smelled odd, not a bad odd, but there was a chemical smell.

I thought about telling Cal about it, but then decided against it.

I wasn't in the mood to argue or have him insinuate I was crazy.

I needed Barron.

The manager that I couldn't stand at one point because he seemed stuck in the 1950s, even though that was before his time, had suddenly become a sanity ally.

I feared that he had disappeared as well. Barron wasn't anywhere to be seen or heard.

Before returning home, I decided to walk around Hawthorne.

Were there any other neighborhoods that were suddenly gone, that were vacant and quiet?

Just when I thought I found a section of town like Factory Three, I'd hear a voice, see movement.

What was I missing? What were we all missing?

I couldn't get it out of my mind.

My obsession kept me out most of the day, and my inability to not talk about it caused another argument between me and Cal that night.

Four hours he was home, and we bickered the whole time.

He insisted everything was getting back to normal, that power would return and that I'd feel silly. The mayor's meeting would enlighten me.

Would the mayor's meeting enlighten me what happened to Factory Three?

It was a warm night and I used the uncomfortable temperature as a reason to sleep on the porch on the glider swing. I just didn't want to be in the same room as Cal.

Why was he so dismissive?

I was fast asleep, comfortable under a thin blanket, when I felt the hand shake me slightly.

Jumping to a sitting position, I thought it was Cal waking me before he went back on beet to say he was sorry we argued again.

But it wasn't.

Surprising me, it was Barron.

"You made this easy," Barron said. "I expected to knock on your door."

I rubbed my eyes. "What time is it?" The temperature had dropped and I brought the blanket closer to me.

"A little before five. I waited until I saw Cal leave."

"Why?"

"Because I need to steal you."

At that second, I was scared. My insights jolted. "Steal me?"

"Not steal you. But have you come with me."

"Oh, good." I exhaled. "I was afraid you were going to Factory Three me."

Very seriously, Barron looked at me. "That's why I need you to come with me."

Barron had thought ahead; he brought a thermos with coffee. I grabbed a cup from my kitchen, a jacket, and left a note for the boys that I was with Barron.

I didn't say where, because I didn't know.

Barron wore a backpack, and had one bicycle with him, which he didn't ride. He walked with it as we both moved about a third mile to the edge of Hawthorne, where he had another one.

The coffee I had been happy about; bikes, not so much.

"Can you ride a bike?" he asked.

"Yeah. Not sure how well in the dark. Why are we out here?"

"Ever since our conversation at the store, and then finding Factory Three, I couldn't sleep. Something is going on."

"Obviously," I said.

"So, I have been looking," Barron said. "I pulled out the map." He reached into his back pocket and handed me a folded map. Then with a swing around of his backpack, he grabbed a flashlight from there.

When he shined the light on the map, I saw he had drawn grid marks. "All this is where I checked."

"I did the same thing in town today. But you went outside of town. It was our conversation."

Barron nodded. "It was. Are we being isolated or are we the only survivors?"

"Did you find answers?"

He shook his head. "Not to that."

"Then to what?" I glanced back to the map and the areas not marked off. "You found something in this area east of Factory Three." I lifted my eyes to look him,

"I did. Well, I think I did. Which makes sense because if an entire portion of town left, they didn't take the main road."

"They took Stewart. But Stewart goes only one way. It ends…"

"At the shoe factory."

For some strange reason, Barron called it paranoia, he didn't want to go back through town to get to the old abandoned shoe factory. We took the long way to Stewart.

That narrow two-lane road led straight to the parking lot, behind the Factory Three housing.

When we arrived it was still dark, but it wouldn't be for long. The edge of the sky started to lighten with the rising sun.

A small field separated the backyards and the lot. I imagined at one time the workers walked across that field after a hard day at the factory, grateful for the short walk to their homes.

I saw the field when we were at Factory Three. It was overgrown with weeds.

But I didn't take a closer look.

Parking our bikes near the end of the lot, it didn't take me long to see what I hadn't seen when I was standing in Factory Three.

"Oh my God," I whispered, nearly stunned off my feet when I saw the clear indication of tired tracks or something that had flattened the weeds in the field.

"They all came from Factory Three through this field," Barron said. "I followed the tracks. There are four of them. Four sets. Big ones. In the center it looks like it stopped. There's a huge flat spot there, maybe the truck stopped for a while."

"We have to wait until light and get pictures," I said. "We have to get pictures and show people."

"We do. I brought the camera."

"When did you find this?" I asked.

"Just before it got dark. I could see then. I wanted you with me to confirm."

"I'm confirming. There are clear tracks from Factory Three to here. Did you check the old factory?"

At that point, we both turned and looked.

"No," Barron replied. "I was kind of scared to."

I glanced down at my watch, then to the sky. "We can't take pictures until it's light, so maybe we can check out the factory then too."

"Good idea."

"For the record, I don't blame you for being scared."

The old factory looked ominous and dark, almost burned out.

We rode the bikes over that way, circling the old factory in search of an entrance that would be easier to get through.

Only one wasn't chained.

It was spooky. I kept reminding myself it would be light soon and that it would look better in the day.

I remembered that at one time it was pristine, workers went in and out of it at all hours, and tried to reassure myself that there was nothing to be afraid of.

But I didn't believe that.

I grabbed Barron's flashlight to examine the door and windows. Worst case scenario, we could climb through one of the windows, after all they were broken.

But what did we expect to find inside? Why were we even there at the factory? The find was in the field. The tire tracks were tangible, but did we really think we'd find everyone from Factory Three inside the old factory?

"I think we should go back toward the field," I told Barron. "We show people the pictures and then let them check the factory."

"You know what, I agree. It could be dangerous."

"We could fall and get hurt," I said.

"No way to the hospital."

"Let's go back to the field and wait." I readied to turn off the flashlight and when I did, the beam swung.

I gasped.

Barron shrieked.

When a man peeked out through the window and the light caught him.

He was as scared as we were.

I wanted to run, but there was a scream, not Barron's. It was the man. It was in the distance and grew closer, louder. A scream of fear, one that was long and shrill.

Just as we were about to back up and run, the door blasted open and the man came out.

He ran full force to us.

"Thank God. Thank God. Thank God. Barron from the store, right?"

"Yes." Barron tried to move back as the man grabbed for him.

"You have to help me. I was hiding," the man said panicked. "Help."

"We will. What's going on?" I asked.

"They're dead." The man pointed. "They're all dead."

TWELVE
TELL THE TOWN

"They're dead, they're all dead."

Something was wrong. Suddenly I went from thinking we were about to find our answer, to being suspicious of this man.

If it were a movie or book, the truth about what happened to the people in Factory Three would happen at the end. Bits and pieces of information would flow in. But this is real life, and there we were on the cusp of sunrise, ready to hear the truth from a stranger that neither I nor Barron knew. And we knew *everyone* that came into the store.

Who was this man?

He didn't smell right. But it wasn't body odor, it was that chemical smell I caught a whiff of in Factory Three.

"Calm down," Barron told him. "Who is dead?"

"Everyone," he replied.

"That's not true, we're alive. And you know me from the story how?" Barron asked, then suddenly snapped his finger. "Oh, hold on. You're Doug. The agoraphobic. Well, maybe not an agoraphobic, but close to it."

I gasped. "That's not nice."

"He knows what I mean. He wouldn't go into the store; I'd bring his groceries to the back. Every week it was a different reason."

"Oh," I sung my words. "Is this him?"

"Yes. Yes." Barron nodded.

Suddenly, I got where Barron was going. The man was delusional.

"And are you two not listening?" Doug asked. "They are dead."

"Who?" I questioned.

"The people I lived around. There." He pointed to Factory Three.

At that point, even if what he was going to say wasn't true, the tire tracks and impressions in the ground were enough to take to town and show Cal.

"I was out walking. I had a dream, a bad one," Doug said. "When I was coming back, I heard the vehicles. They were like nothing I have ever seen."

"What do you mean?" Barron questioned.

"Black, Square shaped, they were loading people into them."

"Who?" I asked. "Military?"

"I don't know, because they were wearing headgear helmets and one-piece suits like I'd never seen before. People were screaming, crying, they took them from their homes. And they drove them through the field. But they stopped. All the vehicles stopped in the middle of the field. I stayed back."

I turned to Barron. The impressions and indentations in the middle of the field. He had guessed that.

"Then what happened?" Barron questioned.

"I couldn't make out the voices, but I could make out the screams."

"Scream?" I asked.

"They came after the sound. Ever watch a movie where they show a silencer on a gun?" Doug questioned. "It was sort of like that. I…I didn't see what happened. I hid. I hid until the trucks moved out. And I stayed hiding until I saw you. Because I was afraid they were gonna do it to the whole town."

"Do *what*?" I grew frustrated.

"Lady, I told you. They're dead. At least half of them."

At that second, I felt like my husband, so full of disbelief. Yes, those in Factory Three had vanished, but dead?

"Did they take the bodies?" Barron asked.

"No. No. They're in the field."

That was the final clue to me that he was wrong. Bodies in the field? Even if Barron didn't see them, surely, he would smell them.

"Barron, didn't you walk this field?" I asked.

"I followed the tracks."

"Did you see bodies?"

Barron shook his head.

"What the hell is wrong with you two?" Doug snapped. "Come on, I'll show you, then we need to tell someone. If they did it once, they'll do it again."

Away from the direction of the tire tracks and indentation, Doug moved with purpose as if he knew exactly where to go.

The sun was already coming up, it was light out and if there were dead people out there, we'd see them.

A part of me felt like we were wasting time. I wanted to tell Barron that we should just get the pictures and take Doug back to town.

A few minutes into the walk, I smelled something.

Cringing, I lifted my hand to my mouth. "It smells like chemicals."

"Ammonia-based," Barron added. "Why are we smelling chemicals?"

"They sprayed it," Doug answered. "They had to. I've been smelling it ever since. I guess it's to mask the smell of the bodies."

Before I could scoff again, dismiss what I believed was a delusional man, I became like Mr. Mosely.

My disbelief was proven wrong.

He parted the weeds like a curtain. "I didn't count them all, but I believe there are thirty-six."

There they were there.

Bodies.

Mainly men. They were laying there, some on top of each other; they looked as if they had been dumped and discarded.

Their bullet riddled bodies were saturated in blood long since dried, and what appeared to be a blue powder. There were no insects, or buzzing flies. Some eyes were open, mouths too. Others had arms reaching as if they weren't dead when they been brought there.

I heard the sound of retching and turned my head to see Barron hunched over, vomiting into the grass.

My first instinct wasn't to scream or run, it was a feeling of confirmation.

Something bigger was happening, and as soon as we let the mayor and others know about the bodies in the field, the missing Factory Three people, I was taking my family and exactly doing what Mr. Mosely had said to.

Leaving and running for the hills.

I knew we needed to get to town as soon as possible; there was no time to trek through the streets between us and Main Street. The fastest way would be as the crow flies. Straight through the fields into Factory Three.

Admittedly, I was a little scared to run through those fields. Would something else be there that we hadn't seen yet?

Before leaving, while Barron pulled his regurgitating self together, I looked at the bodies in the field, I looked because I wanted no chance to reply with an 'I don't know' when the questions started coming.

Thankfully, I didn't see any children there. Upon further looking, I did see women. Mostly older, no young ones. In fact, everyone in that field looked over the age of forty. Then again, it was hard to tell. Some of their faces had suffered major damage.

One thing was consistent. It was that blue powder. It covered them like a light snow dusting.

Doug had counted thirty-six, I counted thirty-three. But it was still a lot.

I didn't have any water for Barron, I wish I had. He looked pale and was glad to get out of there. I made sure I took pictures, and together, we walked cautiously through the field.

Doug stayed behind to make sure no one came and took the bodies. I didn't understand that logic, but there was no time to question him.

As we emerged from the field, surprising me was Mr. Mosely.

He was walking to our left, and when he spotted us, he turned and headed our way.

"I knew you'd be here," he said.

"Were you looking for me?" I asked.

"Yes. Yes, I was. I heard you on the porch with whiz kid, and saw you'd snuck off with him," Mr. Mosley said. "When you didn't come back, I figured it was one of two things. Either you were off having an affair—"

My gasp of offense silenced him. "Oh my God."

"Don't 'Oh my God' me, he came right after Cal left." Mosely pointed at Barron.

"How do you know this?" Barron asked.

"I was on my porch too. Anyhow, after realizing that was a ridiculous notion, since you both discovered Factory Three, I thought maybe you were playing Scooby Doo here." He sniffed. "What is that smell?"

"Me," I replied.

"I know. What is it?"

"Dead bodies."

"I know what bodies smell like; that's not it."

"It's the chemical they used to mask the body smell," I said.

"Who?"

"Whoever did this."

"Did what?" he asked frustrated.

Barron replied. "Killed half the people in Factory Three. We're on our way to tell Cal, the Chief and the Mayor."

"Now, hold on here. Are you saying you found the bodies?"

"We're in a hurry," I said.

"Are they dead?" Mr. Mosely asked.

I grunted. "Yes. I told you this."

"Then they aren't going anywhere. How did you find them?"

I replied, "Doug."

"Who is Doug?"

I tossed up my hands. "Why does it matter?"

"Maybe he killed them," Mr. Mosely raised his eyebrows.

I scoffed. "I highly doubt it. He was hiding, he was scared, he saw it all. Every bit. He's staying with the bodies in case whoever did this tries to take them."

Barron explained, "And Doug is the town partial agoraphobic."

"Oh, the man that goes to the back of your store for his groceries," Mr. Mosely said.

"Can we just leave?" I asked. "We want to report this."

"And you will. I want to check it out first. After you went screaming to Cal in the middle of the street that aliens took the people of Factory Three, I think they may be hesitant to believe you."

"I did no such thing," I defended. "It was nighttime when I told Cal. But fine. Let's go check."

"If you guys don't mind," Barron stated. "I'm going to stay back. I really don't want to see that again."

"You know what?" I spoke. "Go on Mr. Mosely, just follow the tire tracks in the field. You'll see Doug. I'm going to wait with Barron."

"Don't leave and run into town. Wait until I get back."

I nodded and Mr. Mosely walked toward the field.

"We going to run into town?" Barron asked.

"I was thinking that. But you know, let's enjoy the satisfaction of seeing Mosely's face when he comes back and tells us we were right."

It took longer than I expected, though maybe I was just anxious waiting for Mr. Mosely to return.

When he did, he returned alone. Doug wasn't with him. Mr. Mosely didn't have that humble look, he looked disturbed, an expression seldom seen on his stern face.

He looked at us both. "Let's go report this."

There was an unexpected smell of coffee in the crisp morning air, as we made our way toward town.

It was just everywhere, and like an addict, my blood boiled for a good cup. It smelled good. Then I realized were about thirty minutes from the big Mayor meeting.

I just wanted to find Cal, tell him and hope he did something.

I know he didn't agree with me, or thought I was insane about Factory Three. I didn't get why. How could he even think it was absolutely normal for an entire neighborhood to leave? Not pack up and leave, just leave.

As we approached the outskirts of the downtown area, in the small community park, three grills were set up. Old percolator pots were on the grates, and that was where the coffee smell came from.

People were there, waiting, grabbing cups and preparing them with sugar and cream from the coffee condiment table. I would be lying if I said I didn't want to go over there first, but I didn't.

I spotted Cal. He was directing people to seats. A makeshift stage was set up and on top of the podium was a megaphone.

What the mayor had to say must have been a big deal.

Maybe he knew about Factory Three. I doubted it though; the bodies were still out there.

"Mom."

"Mom."

I turned my head and saw Sam and Jake running my way.

They looked so relieved to see me that both of them grabbed me with an embrace.

"Mom," Sam gushed. "I was so worried."

"Me, too," added Jake. "We woke up, you were gone." He then looked at Mr. Mosely. "Thank you for finding her."

"Oh." I sung out the word, turning to Mr. Mosely. "They sent you for me. You acted like you were concerned and went out on your own."

"I was. The boys came for me," Mr. Mosely stated. "We've been out looking."

"Where were you, Mom?" Sam asked. "Why were you with…him?"

"We're not having an affair," Barron said.

Unexpectedly, Sam lunged for him.

"Now. Now, stop." Mr. Mosely blocked Sam. "Calm down. They aren't sneaking off in a fun way. They found something."

"Shelby," Cal angrily spoke my name.

Actually, he didn't have to sound angry, he called me 'Shelby. A mere turn of my head and he was right there.

"Where the hell have you been?"

"Cal, listen—"

"You can't run off with the local frat boy and not tell anyone," Cal snapped. "Where the hell were—"

"Whoa. Whoa. Whoa." Mr. Mosely held up a hand. "Stop. First, she's your wife, don't take that tone. Second. Shel, tell him."

"Something happened at Factory Three," I said. "People, soldiers, I don't know, they came in, took half the town and killed the rest. We found the bodies in the field."

Cal stuttered, "W-what?"

"The bodies of thirty of them are in the field covered with some powder."

Mr. Mosely clarified, "They were all shot and the powder is a chemical I have never seen. There's no sign of decomposition and there is no smell. It has to be the powder."

"Holy crap," Jake exclaimed. "That could have been us."

Cal stood in a state of shock. "This is insane. Are you sure?"

"We have pictures," I said.

"Hold on. I'll get the chief informed and tell the mayor."

Just as Cal stepped away from our group, I felt this vibration beneath my feet. Just a slight vibration.

He kept walking.

Twenty feet from us, my ears felt a pressure. As if something was in them.

"Anyone feel that?"

I didn't get a response. I didn't need to.

A split second later, a roaring began, louder than any thunder I have ever heard. It sounded like engines with a high-end squeal.

It came from above and as me and my sons lifted our heads to see, eight, maybe ten of these black aircraft soared over head of us.

They were in some sort of formation.

My chest filled with a vibration and energy, I found it hard to believe. The sight of these aircraft caused everyone around us to stop.

"What was that?" Sam asked. "What are they?"

"Is that a new jet?" I asked Mosely. "Airforce is being called out."

"Looks it, but it's like nothing I've ever seen," Mr. Mosely said.

Jake said, "Maybe they're a new design."

I saw them. They flew a distance, looking more like birds and then they broke formation and turned around.

"Shit," Mr. Mosely grabbed my arm. "Boys, Shel. Run. Take cover!"

All I could mutter in my confusion was, "What?"

"Reisling Pharmacy. Basement. Now!" Mr. Mosely ordered.

"What?" I asked. "What's happening?!"

"Run, Shel."

Then as he pulled my arm, I saw my sons running toward town square.

Mr. Mosely yanked me to go at the same time, the first sound of gunfire rang out.

Rat-tat-tat.

Rapid gunfire.

Someone was firing at us.

Through my peripheral vision, I caught Barron racing by, catching up to my sons.

I couldn't help it, I had to look up, I had to see. The aircraft were no longer flying in a neat order, but any way they could.

It looked like a mixture of fire with a blue color coming down at us.

Each strike caused the ground to explode, dirt flew up, concrete.

I looked behind me for Cal.

Where was my husband?

We were running in a straight line, then the gun fire hit a car in front of us. Mr. Mosely pulled me to the right.

Again, I looked back.

The mayor was running. Then he was hit. He flew up in the air then slammed to the ground.

I couldn't register it all. Just watching those in my town go down.

"Cal!" I yelled out. I knew he didn't hear me. "Run."

But then he spotted me.

I saw his eyes. He locked on to me.

"Damn it, Shel," Mr. Mosely shouted. "Run faster."

He was right, I had to run. My husband was fine. He was behind us. He was fine.

As I turned to put my focus forward, to run with Mr. Mosely, to catch my sons. I watched as whatever they shot from the plane, came down in a direct hit.

It shot from behind Cal, and blasted straight through his chest.

It sent him flying forward and to the ground.

"No!" I stopped to turn back, to run to him.

I almost was successful, but Mr. Mosely, flung out his arm, wrapped it around my waist, lifted me and turned me to run.

"Damn it, Shel, run!" he repeated.

"Cal!" I screamed.

I was out of it, screaming and hysterical. A state of shock and horror. I don't know how long that lasted, but I know, eventually, I caved.

Gunfire, explosions, people dropping. Blood splattering out with each hit people took. It snapped me into a fight or flight mode, and in order to live, it was flight.

My husband was gone.

My boys had to be safe, but I wouldn't know that unless I kept running to find them.

So, I did what I had to do.

I ran.

THIRTEEN
BAND-AIDS

Making it down to the pharmacy basement was a blur. I thought for sure I was dying. Not from gunfire, but a heart attack. Watching that happen to Cal, seeing him gunned down so brutally destroyed me. I knew my sons didn't know, they were far ahead, thankfully running for their lives.

I didn't know if people heard Mr. Mosely yelling for the boys to get to the basement, but everyone seemed to run there as if there wasn't another basement in town.

I started really running, running away from the gunfire, from the reality that my husband was dead, from everything. The moments were all a blur, but eventually I was in the crowded narrow staircase.

I didn't recall making it through the pharmacy to the back, just being in that dark area, people screaming, and crying, and Mr. Mosely getting irritated.

"Stop it. Quiet! We're under attack. You want them to come for us?" he whispered graveled.

"It's dark, I can't see," a woman cried out.

It was.

Early morning, a brightly lit day, yet, with no power, the basement stairs were dark.

"Feel your way," said Mr. Mosely. "Just feel your way."

I crammed into that stairwell. Mr. Mosely held my arms. I knew that, but I couldn't see whose back was against my chest and who the back of my head was touching.

The fear was thick, draping us all, taking away any calming air.

Then a small hint of light appeared. I couldn't see where it came from. But someone called out to follow the light. And when they repeated it, I realized, it was Sam's voice.

"We'll stay here until you're all down. Follow the light."

What did he find? A candle? Flashlight. He and Jake were the first ones down there. They scrambled through the darkness and found something; I don't know how.

I don't even think my feet touched a step; I was moved by the smashed group of people. The light grew closer and I knew I was almost there.

No one was really quiet, the groans and stifled weeping of people just made for a noisy environment.

Finally, I reached the bottom and lunged for my oldest son. "Where's Jake?"

"Behind you."

I tried not to cry, I wanted to be strong, I turned and hugged my middle child.

"This way." Jake held a light in his hand. It was small and he used it as a guide, moving it back and forth for the benefit of those in the dark. "Everyone this way. There's a big room back here."

"Keep moving," Mr. Mosely said. "Good job, Jake."

I followed my son and his light; it flicked and then went out. That was only briefly, I heard this clicking sound and the light came back on. When it did, I noticed Jake was wounded.

"Where did you get that?" I asked.

"Mr. Mosely."

Moving with the tide of people washed me farther from my sons and into the back room.

I heard that wind-up clicking again, and then Mr. Mosely produced a light.

"I would have pulled this out on the steps, but I couldn't reach my back pocket." He moved people farther into the room, shining his flashlight around. "There's boxes; this is storage. Christmas stuff. We have to look for candles or something. I don't know how long we'll be down here."

He moved his light and it shone on Barron who was already looking in boxes.

"Anything?"

"Nothing, but with the small light, maybe I can find something," Barron replied. "I was just feeling."

I took a deep breath and lifted my eyes to the ceiling, not that I could see anything. Being so consumed with getting below, finding my sons, and the sight of losing my husband, I didn't notice until that second that I could still hear the gunfire and explosions above.

We stood shoulder to shoulder in that room, or at least it seemed that way. If they found us, and it was their intent to kill us, we were sitting ducks.

"We have to keep quiet," Mr. Mosely instructed. "I know what we just went through was horrendous, but we have to not make a sound until it quietens down out there."

The light in the room increased when my boys entered.

Sam quietly closed the door.

Mr. Mosely whispered to me, "I'm gonna secure the back door over there."

I nodded.

"I think I found candles," Barron called out softly. "They smell like it, anyway."

"Mom," Jake said, approaching me and standing close. "Are you okay?"

"Yes," my voice shivered. "*No*. But I will be."

Sam walked over. "We're all in. At least two dozen people."

"It feels like more," I replied.

"Mom, where's Dad?" Sam asked.

Then Jake questioned. "Did he run somewhere else?"

That was all it took. Just one question, and my walls of valor completely crumbled. I brought my hand to my mouth to muffle any noise, trying not to sob too loudly.

"Mom?" Jake asked.

"No," Sam said softly.

"Daddy didn't make it," I choked.

"Are we sure?" Sam asked. "Maybe he got away."

"We should go find him," Jake stated.

"He's gone. He's gone. I saw. I watched."

I wanted to collapse, to release my pain and grief vocally, but I couldn't. The groans of pain that emanated from my children shot through my soul. My sons were so dimly lit, it was a blessing that I couldn't see the expressions on their faces because it would have broken me.

Like chess pieces waiting to be played, none of us moved. My legs cramped, I wanted to sit, but I was fearful. We didn't know if we would have to run out one of the doors.

My sons stood by one, Mr. Mosely by the other. I always knew Mr. Mosely had a handgun. He never hid it, but it never made a difference until I saw him holding it. Usually, it was in his holster snapped to his hip.

There weren't enough bullets in that gun to save us all.

Barron had found these red stick candles that people would put on their Christmas dinner tables, and a lot of us held them to bring some light to the room. I don't know how long we stood there, but it was long enough for the wax to roll over my hand and the candle to get smaller.

Never in my life did I expect to be standing there in the dark basement of the local pharmacy, listening to the sounds of war.

Sure, there had been horror stories, told by my father, about how we always needed to be ready, but to me that was just paranoia of a different generation.

Yet, there we were. Me and my two remaining children cowering in the dark, while both my husband and youngest child had become victims of this unprovoked attack.

Then again, was it unprovoked?

I didn't know what had caused this to happen, nor even really what *was* happening. We had been in the dark nearly a week, and for all I knew, the rest of the world was gone.

It had to be.

We were Hawthorne Kentucky. Before the Youngen Virus, we had a population of thirty-three hundred. A dot on the map barely seen. We couldn't be the target of an attack like this, there was no way.

So, why were the residents of Hawthorne either gone, or hiding in this store room?

Why did our children come down with this virus?

Why did my baby have to die? My husband?

The assault was brutal. We did nothing to deserve it. Then again, war *was* brutal and showed no prejudice on those who died and didn't.

But why us?

There was nothing special about Hawthorne, or was there? Perhaps there was some secret military base or weapons plant that I didn't know about. Something militaristic hidden under the guise of a picture-perfect small town.

Mr. Mosely would know.

I inched my way over to him, being careful not to let my candle go out.

"You alright?" Barron asked, as I passed him.

"Yeah, I'm okay. Thank you." I stood by Mr. Mosley. "Hey," I whispered.

"Hey."

"If there was a secret lab or missile silo under us, you would tell me, right?"

"If I knew, then yes. I don't know of any."

I nodded.

"Wondering why Hawthorne?"

"Yes."

"Me, too," he said. "It doesn't make any sense. And I spent my life in the military. Those jets are like nothing I have ever seen."

"Only two other countries had the ability to create something so sophisticated," I whispered.

"China and Russia."

"Narrowed it down. But why?" I asked.

"Why is a question people ask during war time, and only history gives us the answer. Unfortunately, that will be long after we are gone."

"I know."

"When we get out." He paused, lifted his head, and made sure no one was listening. "We go. We pack up and we leave. We leave at night when it's dark so they can't see us moving. We take it slow, but we go."

"Go where?"

"With all that just happened, I have a few places in mind. We have the supplies to last a while. Even if we have to hide in the woods."

"We'll go where you say."

"I also think we need to keep our assets close. We need to take Barron with us," he said.

"Why?"

"Because he knows how to build things. He's smart, Shel. He can be our professor from *Gilligan's Island*."

Despite my sadness, that made me huff breath that was nearly a laugh.

Mr. Mosely reached out and placed a hand on my shoulder. "I am so sorry about Cal."

"Me, too."

"We'll talk more when we're out of here."

"When will that be?" I asked.

"Soon. I think. Soon. Just listen."

Listen.

I had been.

One thing I listened for but never heard was footsteps. The thought of that scared me. Hearing them above me.

The footsteps never came, and eventually, the gunfire ceased; there were no explosions and the roaring jets overhead were long gone.

Was it time?

Not that I was any sort of expert, but I believed it was. At least take a chance, go up and look.

I was getting ready to suggest to Mr. Mosely that we designate someone—Maybe Barron—but as I did, I heard the creak of the door.

My heart skipped a beat thinking someone was coming in. It wasn't. It was someone going out. And not just someone, my sons.

No. No. No. Not happening.

Despite Mr. Mosely trying to stop me, I plowed through the people. Suddenly my scared self was brave.

It was my children. They were all I had left in the world.

I caught the door just as one of them tried to shut it.

Sam looked in, "Mom, what are you doing?"

"I'm going with you."

"No, stay here."

"No. We stick together."

Sam grunted but reluctantly released the door.

"Keep quiet, keep low," he said.

"Why is she here?" Jake asked.

Seriously? Were my sons questioning my presence as if I were annoying them or showing up to something they were doing with their friends?

"She wants to go."

"Why?"

"Just move," I told them.

I didn't care. I stuck to my guns and followed them, creeping up the steps. Midway up, Sam shut off his light. There was enough light coming from the open door up top to see our way up.

Doing some sort of belly crawl up the stairs, Sam reached the top first. He extended his arm back, signaling us to wait, as he slowly peeked forward to look. After a second, he nodded and inched in.

By the time I reached the top of the steps, both Sam and Jake were on the floor.

Sam mouthed me to stay down, and we scooted on our stomachs across the floor.

I didn't know what was out there; I couldn't hear anything. One of my fears was that my boys would see their father's body. Realistically, I knew it wasn't close, but that fear was still there.

The store was in disarray, things lay toppled from the shelves. But it didn't look like looters had been there, it was more likely panicked town residents trying to make their way to safety.

It surprised me how quiet we were, making our way through the maze of stuff on the floor. I don't know I did it, but I saw a box of bandages in front of me and instead of pushing it away, I grabbed it, as if for some reason we would need them.

It was a strange grab I wasn't sure why I did it.

My heart pounded faster as we drew closer to the door.

Sam led the way to the long check-out counter to the right of the door, and he scooted behind it.

Jake and I followed.

I knew why my son was headed there. The windows behind the counter were not floor length, and they offered an ability to hide.

As he secured his position behind the check-out counter, Sam held up his hand, telling us to stay back.

We did, both staying near the wall.

Fear was an understatement as I watched Sam slowly lift his head to peek out.

Please, I begged in my mind, please don't let them see him. Don't let them shoot my son.

He looked, backed down for a moment, then looked again.

When he slid out of view his eyes closed tightly with a frustrated and pained look on his face.

It took a few seconds; my son was trying to make sense out of something. I knew that look—he got it every time he tried to do algebra.

He ran his hand over his mouth, looked at me and Jake and moved his mouth.

"Still there."

Shit.

After lifting a finger, Sam slowly peeked again.

Damn it Sam, I wanted to yell. *You're pushing it. Stop.*

After that final look, he moved his arm, and motioned his head in a clear indication for us to go back down.

But that last look he took really showed how confused he was.

What did he see?

He led the way again.

I wanted more than anything to look, but I would have to rely on what my son told me.

My purpose for going up with them had nothing to do with seeing what was happening, it was more being a mother, wanting to be there for her children, and there, if God forbid, something happened.

They chivalrously waited for me to get to the basement stairwell first. I went in front and hoped they didn't do anything stupid like run back to the window.

My back ached from crawling and once on the stairs, I stood.

That was when I heard it.

As Sam and Jake made it safely into the stairwell, I knew I wasn't the only one that heard. It was mechanical, a whirling sound accompanied by a clanking. Like some sort of machinery running in a plant.

With a cringing look, Sam pulled the door closed. Something that hadn't been done when we went down before.

He carefully made sure he didn't make a sound, then turned on his light.

"Quiet," he said in barely a whisper.

"What was that noise?" I asked.

Then Jake followed with, "What did you see?"

Sam urged us down the stairs.

113

At the bottom, just before the backroom, Jake asked again. "What did you see?"

Slowly, Sam shook his head. "I don't know. It doesn't make sense."

<><><><>

"Okay," Mr. Mosely spoke softly to Sam. "Just try your best to describe everything you saw."

When we returned, we told everyone that they were still up there. People were scared, and they were confused. I knew they wanted it all to be over, that they wanted to get out and check on their families. So many said they were worried about loved ones that were home. There had to be a sense of guilt as well. Not being there for them when it mattered.

More than anything I knew that feeling, I felt it with Luke.

I left him thinking it was fine when it wasn't.

Just like they all did.

I also felt guilty because I was the only down there with my family.

My son was the center of attention because he looked outside.

"It's hard," Sam replied. "It's hard to explain because it's not like anything I've seen."

"Is it aliens?" Jake asked.

I saw the wincing expression on Mr. Mosely, because sure enough when Jake said that, the murmurs of concern raised in volume.

"Shh," Mr. Mosely hushed. "They're still up there."

"They're not coming in," Sam said. "It's like they aren't looking for people."

"They?" Mr. Mosely asked.

"It's people, I think."

"You think?"

"They weren't aliens," Sam replied. "I mean, they had two arms, two legs, and normal human-sized bodies, but they looked like they were wearing some sort of machinal suit."

Immediately, I looked at Barron.

"What was that about?" Mr. Mosely asked.

Barron replied. "Doug—the one that found the bodies—he said the people that did it weren't dressed like anything he'd seen. He didn't get into details like a mechanical suit, but he was certain he didn't see it before."

"And there was a blue light," Sam stated. "I noticed it. A blue light on the neck of the suit. It flashed. They all had it. I'd say robots, but they weren't flexible; the suits moved almost like clothing, but mechanical. It's hard to explain."

"You did well, son," Mr. Mosely said.

Barron asked, "What do we do?"

"Well. We wait," Mr. Mosely replied. "If these are the same people that hit Factory Three, then they leave. We keep checking until they're gone. Eventually they'll move on. Until then," he said. "We just wait."

FOURTEEN
STAY HIDDEN

It took until that night for them to leave.

We sent someone up to check every hour. Usually, they'd come back with some food or a beverage that they'd managed to scavenge, which we were all thankful for.

We were down in that dark basement for around twenty hours, but it felt so much longer than that.

It also felt as if there were a lot more people in that room than there were. There were twenty-three of us in total, including me, my sons, Mr. Mosely and Barron.

By evening, we'd all resigned ourselves to being stuck there for the night; there was some peace in accepting that though, and soon we had all relaxed enough to sit down. It had been a long day, with a lot of hours of standing.

I was afraid to sit.

When I did, I couldn't fall asleep. My sons weren't talking about their father, but I knew that conversation would come. I could tell it was on their minds, they just weren't saying anything.

They were young, they had to be scared. It was a situation none of us ever imagined ourselves in. Even in our most sci-fi themed fears.

Finally, Sam went up for what would be the last time. We suspected they had gone hours earlier, but we just wanted to make sure before we left.

"Here's the plan," Mr. Mosely said to me. "When we get out of here, we head back to our houses and start packing things up. I'll map out a route. Before I do, I'll reach out on the radio, maybe someone, somewhere has a place for us. We rest up in shifts leave when it's dark."

"What about Cal?" I asked. "We can't leave his body in the street. I can't."

"I know. We'll figure that out once we locate him. Okay?"

I nodded.

"Why don't you talk to Barron? Let him know the plan."

"You haven't?" I asked.

"I thought being that you're his sort of friend, it would be better coming from you, and we stand more of a chance of him coming along."

"You really think he's that much of an asset?" I questioned. "He manages a store."

"Remember that 'most likely' he got in high school? He had a scholarship to MIT, that just doesn't happen unless you are super smart, ahead of your time even."

"You know, I never really thought about how much of a shame it was for him to give that all up. It had to hurt."

"Shows a lot for his character. But…in this world now, he'll thrive."

I looked over to Barron who was fussing with something in his hand. "I'll go talk to him."

"Good girl."

I didn't really stand up, more of a scoot and crawl over to him.

"What are you working on?" I asked as I reached Barron's side.

"A radio I found upstairs."

"Did you get batteries?"

He just looked at me.

"Of course you did," I said. "So, listen." I inched closer. "We need to leave town."

"I know."

"Mr. Mosely has an escape plane. He wants you to come with us."

"Really?"

"Yes. He wants to leave at night."

"Where are we going?" Barron asked.

"Not sure, but it's Mr. Mosely, so it'll be safe."

"Thank you," he said.

"So maybe head home, get what you need and meet us back at my place?"

"I'll just go with you. I have nothing really to get. Unless you want me to contribute food and stuff."

"No." I shook my head. "We're fine. Are you sure?"

"Yeah, but I'm not sure you guys want me."

"Of course we do. Why wouldn't you think so?"

"I swear, I am bad luck with these attacks. Like, I'm causing them or something."

I laughed for a second, then realized he was serious. "Why would you think *that*?"

"The grocery store, I was there. Factory Three, I was there the night before, dropping off some rice and batteries."

"Ah, that was nice of you."

Barron shook his head. "Lot of good it did. Look what happened to them. Then I was in town when the attack came."

"It's not following you."

"It is."

"Then tell me connection, you a twenty-something-year-old man, has to the Youngen Virus?"

"A week after you lost your son, a few days before it all went down here in town, I went to my cousin's Bar Mitzvah. Thirty thirteen-year-olds all there. All but two are gone."

"Oh, Barron, these are all coincidences, I can say almost the same—"

"Guys." Sam came into the room. "We can go up."

Everyone stood, and as I rose to my feet, I stopped Barron. "As I was saying, *coincidence.* I'm glad you're coming with us. I'll feel safer."

"Really?"

"Really."

"Thank you."

It was crazy where his mind was going, then again, how many of us blamed ourselves for things that were truly out of our control.

It was human nature. Just as it was human nature to survive.

We did.

We survived the night and I was going to do everything in my power to make sure we kept on surviving.

<>< ><><>

Despite the destruction, and the fires that had burned during the night, the sun was still exceptionally strong, and the sky was clear.

I was tired, as we all were.

We staggered quietly through the store, making our way to the main entrance. I stayed close to my sons, holding Jake's hand.

Mr. Mosely kicked the glass by the door to make a path and, holding his handgun, looked out. When he saw it was clear, he signaled us.

I knew we had to walk through town to get to the street that led us home.

I knew we had to face the carnage.

There were at least a hundred people who had been waiting on the mayor's speech. Those were words we would never hear now.

I braced myself for what I would face.

Stepping out into the street there was broken glass, burnt-out cars, buildings that had been blasted apart. There was evidence of fires that had smoldered all night.

So much destruction in our beautiful town.

But there was one thing that was missing.

The people.

Two dozen of us made it into the basement. I personally witnessed at least a dozen people, including the mayor and Cal get shot, yet there were no bodies.

None.

Was that what the invaders were doing? Moving bodies? Taking them?

There was blood, there was evidence, but not a single body remained.

"Where did he get shot?" Sam asked. "Where did Dad die?"

"Over there." I pointed to the over-turned coffee station.

Sam and Jake ran over.

They looked. I watched them search. They, along with others, desperately looked for people. Then I noticed Mr. Mosely crouching close to the ground near where I believed Cal was killed.

I walked over to him.

"Did you find something?" I asked.

"You said the bodies in the field had this blue powder?"

"Yes." I nodded.

He lifted his hand, palm facing me. His fingertips were covered in a blue substance.

"They covered them then moved them?" I asked.

Mr. Mosely nodded and sniffed the substance. "It's a chemical I don't recognize. But it's everywhere." He dusted off his hands and stood. "They covered and cleared them. The question is why? Why take the bodies?"

"They didn't take the bodies from Factory Three," I said. "They moved them."

"Then they have to be somewhere."

"Maybe in the field," I replied, then noticed Sam crouching down toward the powder. "Sam, stay away from that."

Mr. Mosely continued. "Why move them into one place?"

Barron chimed in. "Maybe to destroy them all at once."

Mr. Mosely nodded. "Okay, so why the blue powder?"

"I've got a sample already," Barron said. "We can test it. From first guess, it might just be to cover the smell."

"Or maybe—" I stopped talking and jumped back when a huge flame shot up by my feet. "Sam, what the hell?!"

"It's dry gas," he said. "The smell tipped me off; it doesn't smell like gasoline. But why put the bodies together and dust them with it, if it isn't a means to get rid of them?"

I saw the matches in his hand and quickly took them. "You could have been burned."

"Good thinking though," Mr. Mosely stated. "But all this bears another question. If they gathered the bodies to put together to burn them, then why?" he asked. "Why if they are killing us are they getting rid of the bodies?"

"Easy," Barron replied, with a shrug. "They're moving in."

SECOND PHASE

FIFTEEN
LAST NIGHT

The fires burned bright with a lot of blue sparks. There was very smoke and no smell.

Mr. Mosely said there was nothing more sickening than the smell of burning flesh. Yet, we had none of that.

It was almost as if they, whoever 'they' were, knew we were coming to search for our loved ones.

Those of us in the basement had barely made it to Factory Three when we saw the flames shooting up.

My sons had kept their strength until that moment.

They raced forward like many others, trying to get close, to see, but the heat and fire was too intense.

Jake screamed out his anger and pain, Sam wept.

They realized, as did I, that we would never know if Cal was in that field.

Forever they would live with the uncertainty of their father's death. I knew he was dead. I saw. The hole in his torso told me my husband hadn't survived. But the boys didn't see, so they couldn't accept it, no matter what I.

We retreated back to our street to start preparations for leaving.

Half of those in the basement went to their homes to look for loved ones, the other half followed us, as if Mr. Mosely was some sort of guru in survival that could protect them all. I could tell by their faces they felt safer around him.

I didn't blame them.

So did I.

But Mr. Moseley didn't want that honor or responsibility. I wondered how he would handle leaving in the only working automobile.

Would he just abandon everyone?

The nine that remained camped out on his lawn and mine.

My boys moved slowly and I didn't push them. They didn't have the momentum they needed, yet they packed items into boxes and carried them to Mr. Mosely's house.

Barron worked on something on my back porch. He tore apart that radio he found at the pharmacy, one of those cheap jobs, and its pieces lay neatly on the table beside him. He asked if I had another radio or something with a speaker. I gave him what I had and even showed him the old stereo that belonged to my father that was in the garage.

He was excited, and said he would make it work.

I gathered what I could, taking that grocery cart that still remained outside of the Dearling home and using that to carry supplies.

Like my sons, I didn't have momentum. I was drowning in grief over losing my husband and son, and feared beyond reason losing another child.

I had to make them my focus.

Sam and Jake.

By mid-afternoon, I thought our basement followers had scattered, but it seemed they were out scavenging.

I was no leader, yet they approached me as if I were the assistant to the one that would save us all.

"I got tents," one man said. "We'll need tents."

Another stated she got sleeping bags, while another talked about the lanterns.

My favorite was being told by Jurgen Hollow that he taken all the stocked booze from the Dearling home since they left.

Did they leave or were they part of the many casualties in the town square?

I hadn't seen anyone else but us, but that wasn't to say no one else was alive.

With everyone gathering things, I realized they had heard Mr. Mosely talk about his plan.

His garage was locked and so was his front door. I went around to the back, glancing over at Barron.

"I'm almost there," Barron said. "I think I may have it."

"Good." I gave a thumbs up, not really knowing what he was building.

I knocked on Mr. Mosely's kitchen door, and decided to give him a minute before I entered. But I didn't need to wait. Without saying a word, he opened the door, and waved his hand for me to follow. And follow, I did.

It was the first time I had been in Mr. Moseley's kitchen; it was old fashioned almost as if he hadn't changed a thing since his wife passed.

He walked down the hallway of his one-story house, turning into the first room. In there he had cases and he proceeded to load guns into them. The entire room looked like a museum.

"Holy cow," I said. "You have a lot of guns."

"Treasures," he replied. "I collect them. Some of them are from World War Two."

"Do they work?"

"I clean and check these weapons once a month. They work," he said. "We'll need them all, and you're going to learn how to shoot."

"Okay."

"Good."

"Mr. Mosely."

He slammed the case lid. "Why do you call me that? Can't you call me John?"

"No."

"Well, alright then."

"Mr. Mosely, there are a lot of people out there gathering supplies. I think they think they're coming with us."

"Then they come with us," he said.

"We all can't fit in your car."

"With all the supplies, we were never fitting in the car," he said. "I'll drive at a walking pace, keeping it slow, and I won't turn on the lights, so not to attract attention to us." He glanced to his watch, then looked outside the window at our new travel companions. "If they're coming, they'd better get some rest."

"I'll tell them. What else do you need me to do?"

"Well, you might want to think about feeding everyone. There has to be some extra supplies. Gotta get used to feeding a lot of people."

"I'll work on that," I replied. "Do you know where we're going? Do you have a destination?"

"A couple places, yes. After I finish this, I am going to hit the radio again, see if I hear anything."

"Barron is working on something."

"Good. Maybe he's working on a transceiver so we can call out."

"Wouldn't that require a microphone?" I asked.

"It would."

"He's not working on one of those. I'll suggest it though."

"Good."

"I'll leave you be." I turned, and when I did, I saw the wall by the door. I hadn't noticed it when I walked in. It was pictures, all of them featured his son. They went from a baby to an adult male wearing a navy uniform. Slowly, I turned back toward him. "Mr. Mosely?"

"Yes."

"Do we want to try to find your son?"

"No," he answered quickly.

Just as I was about to ask why, Mr. Mosely told me.

"My son, Roger, he...passed away four years ago. On duty."

He said the words stoically, as if he'd repeated them a million times before.

I was absolutely floored.

"I had no idea; I am so sorry," I spluttered.

"Well, I didn't say anything."

"I'm *so* sorry."

"I am too."

I started to leave but stopped. "Why didn't you say anything?"

"Because of that look you're giving me. I hate seeing it."

"Understood."

As I left that room, I realized we were terrible neighbors. I didn't even know he had lost his son. How horrible for him. His wife, his only child, and yet he went on.

I had a lot more to learn from Mr. Mosely than I had first thought.

"My fellow Americans."

It wasn't a clear signal, and there was a lot of static, but it was the president of the United States speaking. It was the first I had heard anything from him in days. Earlier, he had given addresses about the Youngen Virus and how he had all the best minds in the world working on it.

A part of me believed he succeeded because it stopped.

Then came the blackout.

Mr. Mosely picked up a repeated message stating the president would address the nation. That was just before Mr. Mosely was ready to pack up the radio and battery, because we were set to leave, but he held off so we could hear the speech.

We all gathered around it to listen.

"My fellow Americans, I speak to you now from a secure location. One I will keep secret in case our enemies are listening. Our enemies. I can assure you at this moment, we do not know who they are, but we will find out. There is global radio silence. There has been talk that our invaders may be from farther away than we can comprehend, but I assure you, their technology, while advanced, *is* from this earth. Today was a day of brutal attacks upon our soil in countless cities and towns. While the Vice President, his family, and the First Lady and I are all safe, I assure you we cannot bear, as you do, the full impact of this tragedy."

Come on, I thought, *say something, give us something.*

"We all feel it," the President said. "This is our home. We will not stand for this. We are tracking their aircraft as I speak to you, and I promise you that we will fight. But we cannot do this alone. Just as our forefathers fought for our freedom, you must rise up with us. It will take all of us together. We Americans are slow to anger. We always seek peaceful avenues before resorting to the use of force, but now is the time for force. I fear the worst is yet to come, but the we will prevail. I promise you that, America. Stay safe. Stay vigil. God bless you."

Static.

"Well." Mr. Mosely shut off the radio. "Nice speech but nothing we don't already know."

"What do you think he meant by the worst is yet to come?" I asked.

Mr. Mosely only looked at me, then as he disconnected the radio. He said, "It's time to get to the hills and woods."

I nodded in agreement, hating but ready to say goodbye to the home I had known for so long. Everyone started to disperse and I heard Barron calling out as he ran toward us.

That was when I realized he wasn't there for the president's speech.

"I got something," Barron said. "I got something."

"Is it something that can wait?" Mr. Mosely asked. "We're getting ready to leave."

"I'd like you of all people to take a listen," Barron said.

"Sure thing." Mr. Mosely walked behind Barron, and I stayed close as well. I was curious as to what he was doing on my back porch.

He had been there all day and night.

On my patio table, he had that pharmacy radio, hooked up with wire and to a speaker. Jake sat in the chair, staring at the speaker. I noticed one wire ran from the radio to the awning above my patio.

"What is that wire?" I asked and pointed.

"Sort of like a satellite dish." Barron looked at Jake. "Still there?"

"Yep." Jake stood.

Mr. Mosely asked, "Did you make a transceiver?"

"Um, no, not yet. That's easy," Barron said. "I wanted to finish this."

"What is it?" Mr. Mosely asked.

Barron sat down. "If I were the enemy and I wanted to communicate with my planes and ground troops, I would want to do it on a frequency those I was attacking couldn't pick up."

"I'm sure the government is searching every known frequency."

"*Know*," Barron wagged his finger. "Is the key word. I was trying to pick up something that was hiding. And I got it. First, this is what I heard."

A song, smothered in static and distortion played. I recognized it.

I watched Mr. Mosely blink a couple times. "David Bowie, Changes, 1972."

Barron nodded. "Exactly."

Jake added. "There are others that play. They sound almost sour, right? Like the batteries are dying."

Mr. Mosely shook his head. "Okay, why do we care?"

"It's a message," Barron said. "This is the enemy. They know us. They're sending us a message to decipher."

"Through a David Bowie song?"

"And Bob Dylan," said Jake.

"Boys, I appreciate your eagerness," Mr. Mosely said. "Picking up music is not picking up the enemy."

"Nope. It's not," Barron said. "I think the songs are a hint. They're being clever. They're a message, not just a veil or masking."

"What are you talking about?" Mr. Mosely asked.

"Listen." Slowly, Barron moved his homemade dials and the music faded exposing a high-pitched beeping, a tone that was different, but there.

"When I asked Jake if it was still there," Barron said. "This signal is what I meant. It repeats, it has patterns."

"Holy Cow in a crossroads," Mr. Mosely said. "How did you find this?"

"Accident. Honestly, when I found the songs, I was just trying to tune it better and the signal appeared."

"It's not Morse Code." Mr. Mosely leaned forward, listening. "I know Morse Code. But it is some sort of code."

Barron nodded. "We just need to crack it."

"Can you?"

Barron sighed out. "I'm more electronics, but we can all try. We need to study it."

"We also need to get on the road. Pack it up, make a plan," Mr. Mosely said. "And Barron. Excellent job."

When Mr. Mosely left, I looked at Jake and Barron excitedly, exchanging celebratory glances.

I was amazed at what they found. Was it really a code of sorts used by the enemy?

It was foreign to me, then again so were our invaders. I knew it would probably take a long time to crack that code, but if we did, maybe just maybe we could find out who was attacking us and more importantly, why my family and so many others had to die.

SIXTEEN
MOVING OUT

Mr. Mosely wanted to be on the road at exactly 11 p.m. He estimated it would take us six hours of walking to get to a point that would be safe enough for us to stop and rest.

At first, I didn't understand, especially as he drove his car like a pied piper out of Hawthorne, to the back roads. One after another, we followed him. It was shortly after midnight that our convoy inched our way onto Hathaway Road, or as the maps had it, Route 536. A heavily treelined roadway that would take us to Florence. At least that's what I thought. He had mentioned that before.

Florence wasn't that far, but we were moving slow. We all stayed together, following Mr. Mosely as he drove at a snail's pace, leading us all.

A part of me wished I'd pulled out a map and looked for myself. But then what choice did we have?

Our town was hit, and chances were, many others had been hit as well.

The president didn't mention much, which was a disappointment. Maybe he just didn't know or maybe he was afraid to tell us.

I wished, with everything I was, that I had a clear view of a plan. Where we would go, what we would do.

The truth of the matter was, we were now war refugees just trying to get to some place safe.

I would imagine Hawthorn would have been one of those places. But it wasn't. We were not immune to any of it.

How much around us had been hit or destroyed that they were now going after no name small towns?

In the short time of the blackout, had they hit every major metropolis? I always imagined if faced with something like this, we would know. We would be aware.

But we weren't.

Once everything went dark, so went the information.

Moving without direction, following an old beat-up car that ran because its owner had the foresight to stock parts and the knowledge to know how to get it running.

No one said anything as we moved; there was no talking, just walking.

There were no planes in the sky, no sounds of explosions.

Mr. Mosely would stop his car once an hour for a few minutes to give everyone a chance to rest. It seemed as if we were walking forever.

The sky was clear and the moon drifted, telling me we had been at it for hours,

Finally, just before four in the morning, Mr. Mosely put on his blinker and pulled over.

I was more toward the middle of the line of people behind him, and when I made my way to his car, I saw the sign on the right. The sign was buried in the darkness as was the single gravel road itself.

Ridge Campground.

"We're going to check it out," Mr. Mosely said. "Not sure if there are people here or not, but it's a good place to stop and hide for a while to rest before we head south."

"We're not going to Florence, are we?"

Mr. Mosely shook his head. "To quote your husband, what is twelve miles? It's still too close to Cincinnati. But if we tell people we want to go farther, it might take the wind from their sails. I'll talk to them. But after we rest."

We all stayed behind Mr. Mosely's car as he drove very slowly up the extremely dark road. The moon and the stars were blocked by the trees.

It was such a dangerous road, it felt like we were walking in nothing but black, like a void of sorts.

Finally, he placed on his headlights until he reached the top of the hill. I assumed we were there. He shut them off, drove a bit more then stopped the car.

He stepped out with a flashlight, went to the back of his car and retrieved a rifle.

"I'm going to go check it out," he said. "Stay put."

"Want me to come," asked Sam.

"That would be great. Thank you." Pulling his handgun from his holster, Mr. Mosely handed it to Sam.

Did he just give my teenage son a gun?

It worried me. Weren't there any other able bodied grown men that could go with Mr. Mosely. I worried as they moved in the direction of the camp, guided by a dim flashlight.

"I should have gone with them," commented Jake.

"No, you shouldn't have." I exhaled, feeling a wave or worry crash into me.

I looked around. Other than Barron, there were six other men. Most of them my age or older. Jurgen Hollow was older than Mr. Mosely, so, he was out. One was even a firefighter; his name I couldn't recall, but he was able bodied, grown. Why couldn't he do stuff instead of my child?

Perhaps it was what Sam wanted to do. If Cal were alive, and with us, he would have been first to go with Mr. Mosely. Probably complaining about his cracked windshield.

We waited for a good twenty minutes. In my imagination the camp was either farther than they thought…or they ran into trouble.

I was almost at the point where I was going to go into Mr. Mosely's trunk, take one of those guns I didn't know how to use, and go find them.

Then they returned.

I didn't even realize I was holding my breath until it all escaped me in the form of one huge exhale.

"It's clear," Mr. Mosely said. "Looks like it's been closed and hadn't opened up for the season. Four small cabins, a latrine, and room for tents. We had to break the locks on the doors to check, but they're clear and dusty. I'd caution lighting a fire because it's a pretty big clearing. No camouflage."

He returned to his car, got in, and drove forward.

The campsite wasn't far at all, a few hundred yards. There was a fence, a check-in office and down the path the four cabins Mr.

Mosely had mentioned. They weren't much bigger than an out-house.

I peeked in one, each had two sets of bunk beds and a dresser.

It was brighter in the open area, with the stars and moon illuminating the clear sky. I was exhausted, but opted not to sleep in the cabins. My boys shared one with Jurgen and the firefighter whose name I didn't recall. Even tired, I was restless. I asked if anyone needed anything.

No one really did.

When I said goodnight or at least Good 'nap' to my sons, I took one of those bottles of vodka that Jurgen had swiped from the Dearling.

I needed the drink. My body was sore and my soul felt broken.

With Jurgen's alcohol generosity, came words of wisdom. "You've been walking, you're tired, probably hungry and you're emotionally spent. Don't drink too much. We don't need you passing out."

"I won't."

Using one of those paper cups people put in their bathrooms, I poured some vodka in there, capped the bottle and sipped as I walked to Mr. Mosely's car.

He was at the trunk checking things. Probably all those damn weapons.

"Drink?" I asked.

"Um." He stared at the bottle and thought about it. "Not right now. Maybe after we settle. Wanna keep my wits. Are you okay?"

"No. No I'm not, but I don't have a choice in what to do."

"Well…" He looked past me to the cabins. "I think everyone here lost someone today. Jurgen's wife was at the meeting. Right at the coffee table. Ray's too."

"Who is Ray?"

"One of the longest surviving firefighters in Hawthorne."

"Ah, that's his name. I couldn't remember."

"Just saying you're all in the same emotional boat."

I finished my little cup of vodka, then poured another. "Then *why*, if we're all in the same boat, does my teenage son always seem to be the one, other than you, to take risks?"

"Because he wants to. Let him. I was his age when I joined the service. I saw combat."

"These are different times," I said.

"Oh, yeah, they are. He's defending his home. Protecting his family. He needs to do this. And don't ask me to ask Barron. I need him on that contraption he made." Mr. Mosely turned and nodded at Barron who sat at a picnic table. His invention was before him.

"Where did he get the old headphones?"

"Me."

"Did he get your transceiver working? It looks like it has a microphone."

"It does but he didn't," said Mr. Mosely. "And right now sending out signals may not be the best idea. He's just using it to listen so he doesn't drive all of us nuts with David Bowie and Bob Dylan."

"Do you think he's right, that the songs are a hint to the signal beneath it?"

"I don't know. Who is going to confirm it?"

140

"I'm going to go talk to him." I lifted the bottle. "You sure you don't want one."

"I'm sure. And don't drink too much. We don't want you passing out."

"I won't. I promise." Bottle and cup in hand I walked over to Barron. "Drink?"

"No, I'm good thanks."

"How's it going?'

Barron grunted.

"Am I bothering you?"

"No. I'm frustrated."

I noticed a notebook was open and there was writing in it. "Are you making progress?"

"No." He shook his head. "I'm trying to write all the lyrics down, I really think if I can find a connection, they are a hint to deciphering this signal."

"Can I ask why they would give hints? I mean, what would be the point?"

"If they were just trying to hide the signal, why play the same three songs?"

"Three?" I asked. "I thought there were two."

"I caught a third one."

"What is it?"

"That's the kicker. I don't know it. I never heard it, and we hear a lot of songs at the store."

"Is the signal still there?"

"Absolutely. I tried to apply Morse Code to it and it's gibberish, so it's definitely not Morse Code."

"Mr. Mosely said that."

"I know," he replied.

After finishing my drink, I pulled his notebook closer. It was hard to read in the dark.

"But really, why give a hint? If the answer is in the music, why do that? Are they playing a game with us?"

"No. I think someone out there is trying to help us, warn us."

"You really think so?"

"I do. Because they know it's going to be bad. I know things are going to get bad. Hell, just the song titles tell me that. Changes? David Bowie. Yeah, things are changing."

"And what's the Bob Dylan song?" I asked.

"Eve of Destruction."

Hearing that was a gut punch. It took me a second to catch my breath. "They're playing, they aren't hinting, that's blunt. They're letting us know they're destroying us."

He hummed and grimaced, facially showing his disagreement. "I'd say yeah, you're right, but the songs are almost as hidden as the signal." He looked down to his notebook. "I'm not being rude, but I want to get back to this." He lifted the headset to his ear.

"I understand. Try to get some rest." I poured another drink as I stood.

"I will, you too, and…" He pointed. "Watch the drinking. We don't need you to pass out."

"I won't but, if I do?"

"You won't be as alert."

"Got it." I wished him luck then walked away. I found one of those folding lounge chairs sun bathers used and I made that my bed just outside the cabin where my sons were sleeping.

I checked on the first before I got comfortable.

It had to be pushing five, the sun would be rising soon and I needed to sleep. I didn't know when we were leaving or if we were leaving.

The campground was a nice hideout; it felt safe.

Using a jacket as a blanket, I reclined back, sipping my vodka and watching the sky.

I really was exhausted, and even though I only had three, maybe four of those little drinks, I was a lightweight. Whether it was exhaustion or the booze, I did what they told me not to do.

I passed out.

<><><><>

My head pounded, its internal percussion thrumming louder than any of the chatter from the camp.

I didn't know what time it was, and I had to really focus to see my watch.

Surprisingly, I had been asleep for three hours. When I did pass out, I didn't feel like I was drunk or even tipsy, but certainly my dehydration-induced aching head was saying otherwise.

I really didn't have my wits about me and it took me a second to even remotely come to my senses. In the moments of waking all I could think of was Cal, and all I could see was him being shot right in front of me.

Get it together, I told myself.

I swung my legs over the lounge chair and rubbed my eyes again, lifting the tipped over, yet capped, bottle of booze.

I glanced around the camp.

My sons were by the other picnic table with Mr. Mosely and a few others.

I could hear that distinctive radio sound. Static, interference and voices. They all looked so concerned.

What did I miss?

What was happening?

I shuffled my way over there, the milk gallon jug with water was on the table and when I arrived, I poured a glass and downed it.

"Mom, are you okay?" Sam asked.

I nodded. "What's going on? What are they saying?"

Jake shook his head. "We're not sure. It's bits and pieces."

"Of?" I asked.

Barron then came over. "All packed up and covered," he told Mr. Mosely. "I buried the battery like you said. Maybe you should disconnect that."

"Yeah. You're right." He shut it off and unhooked the car battery. After covering the battery with a small blanket, he handed it to Barron. "Put that in near the other."

"What's going on?" I asked. "What did I miss?"

Mr. Mosely answered. "About thirty minutes ago we picked up an exchange between our guys. We think they're our guys. Barron found it."

"What were they saying?"

"Controls were down. Barron said he heard the word 'hacked,'" Mr. Mosely said. "That didn't concern me as much as hearing tracking and interception…and that we launched."

I was confused, maybe it was the hangover or just being tired. "If we launched, we're fighting. We know who is doing this. Why shut down the radio?"

"I want to hear more, but I don't want to lose our ability. Remember when the power went out?" Mr. Mosely asked. "This could be the same thing. Possibly worse. Tracking, interception, hacking. All screams to me that our defense systems are scrambled by the enemy."

"But our offense wasn't, right?"

Mr. Mosely waved his hand. "Nothing we heard was full sentences. It was cutting out. Give her your thoughts Ray."

Ray? Who was Ray? I turned and looked. *Oh, yeah, the fire-fighter.*

"Call it crazy, but what if," Ray said. "What if the enemy scrambled everything? Our defenses are down. What if we didn't launch an offensive, but they launched ours for us?"

"Launched what?" I know I sounded dumb when I said that because I saw everyone just looking at me.

And then it hit me.

Missiles.

"No. No. If they want our land, it's not the way to do it. We launch, others will launch to retaliate."

Mr. Mosely tossed up his hands. "Worst case scenario, they launched twenty, thirty minutes ago. Only one other country has the capabilities to launch a full-scale defensive to match ours. If that's the case, in about forty-five minutes we're all in trouble."

I refused, absolutely refused to believe it would come to that.

The enemy had initiated ground forces, there was no reason to set off missiles. They had the upper hand unless we were finally fighting back.

Even then, weren't their people on our soil?

To me it was a bunch of overreacting to scattered and panicked talk, that could or could not be our armed forces.

My head hurt; I didn't want to deal with outlandish speculation, that was just scaring everyone.

Why hide the batteries? Take a few minutes, and listen to it a little more.

Just as Barron returned, I realized I was the fool.

I was unrealistic.

It wasn't what anyone said, it was confirmation that Mr. Mosely, Barron, Ray and everyone else was right.

It came in the form of a flash.

No noise, not at that second, but I didn't need to be some highly educated military guru to know what the flash meant.

It was all white, encompassing, silent and bright. In fact, it was probably my imagination that I could see through my son like an Xray.

"Don't look up," Mr. Mosely instructed. "Look down."

I did. We all did.

A few seconds after the light, I heard the crack. It wasn't like an explosion like I would expect, but it was loud. It was followed by the slight vibration of the ground.

Immediately, panicked voices filled the air.

"Should we take cover?"

"Oh my God, are we going to die?"

"Run."

"Stop." Mr. Mosely held up his hand, using a stern voice. "Just hold on. We saw the flash, heard the explosion, felt a vibration. No blast winds. It's at least fifteen miles from here."

I watched as he walked off in a direction away from the cabins and I followed him. It didn't take long for him to stop. He did and just stood there, arms at his side. We were on top of a pretty big hill and as I joined him, I saw it.

In the distance, there was a mushroom cloud, still engulfed in flames, burning wherever it was. I knew what it was, I had seen pictures of them.

My entire being trembled in fear over what I was witnessing.

"What now?"

"It's north," Mr. Mosely replied. "Cincinnati. It's a good thing we left last night."

"What do we do now?"

"Radiation moves with the jet streams and wind," he said. "We'll catch some of it. The heaviest of it will come in about a half hour. I can't begin to even guess what or how much radiation we'll be exposed to, but for twenty-four hours being outside is taking a big risk."

"Okay, again, what do we do?"

"We have a choice. We can try to go now, probably would take us a couple hours to get to the next town and find a basement, or we block out the windows in the cabins here and hope for the best."

"Which way puts us in the least amount of danger?"

"Staying, but we don't know how much we'll get hit with. If we stay, we have a half hour before it gets here."

"Are you sure?" I questioned. "Are you sure there's going to be radiation here?"

"Positive. How much is the question. I mean, we can get minimal and if that's the case, walking is safe. But we don't know, because I don't have anything to measure it with."

"Alright. We're a group, we put it to the group. Whatever they decided as a majority, we do."

Mr. Mosely nodded. "I usually don't believe in majority rules with life-or-death situations, but this whole thing is a flip of a coin. So, putting it to the group is a good idea. But we need to do it fast."

"Agreed," I said. "Mr. Mosely, was that fast for a counter attack. I mean maybe Russia launched first."

"I don't think those are Russia's nukes. The radio voices said we launched. I believe we did," Mr. Moseley said. "But I also believe the nuclear weapon that exploded on our soil was our own."

SEVENTEEN
AND SO IT BEGINS

A puff of dust came down from the ceiling, causing tiny particles to land in my half cup of coffee.

"Again?"

"They're moving stuff," said Barron. "You heard the general."

I grumbled and turned my attention back to Barron and the small office that they had given us four days earlier.

At first, we stayed at the campsite, blocked the windows, and whiz kid Barron created something called a Kearny Fall Out Meter—it measured radiation. When Mr. Mosely asked how he knew how to do that, he laughed and said it was his science fair project in seventh grade.

Basic stuff.

It wasn't. But we had to rely on it. According to Barron, radiation levels were low, so as a group, we decided to move on after one full day. We packed up, keeping covered with old blankets we found at the camp, and then moved on foot back down to that mountain road.

There was no ash on the road, no fallout, which was a good sign. The wind was taking it in a different direction.

But it was a good thing we left when we did.

Had we left one half hour earlier or later, that clunky, out-dated, awful gold-color pick-up truck would never have spotted us. Of course, we were hard to miss, but it was timing.

The soldier, Kevin, had left the compound to get his grandmother who lived four miles past the Ride Campground driveway.

Clearly, we weren't there when he drove up, but on his way back, he spotted us.

Timing.

Kevin told us that he knew his grandmother, in her secluded home, was safe from the ground attacks, but when the nuclear weapons started to detonate, he couldn't take a chance. He knew that eventually, fallout from the west would arrive.

We were just hours from it reaching us.

The levels weren't skyrocket high, but they were increased enough that we'd all be sick after walking in it for two hours.

Kevin put as many of us as he could fit in his truck, and the rest crammed into Mr. Mosely's car. We had to resort to holding things on our laps, but we all got in.

We drove an hour to a high school in some small town, nestled in the valley of some mountainous ridges. It didn't even have a main street, just a few businesses at a crossroads intersection.

The high school looked like it had been abandoned for longer than the war had been going on, and looks weren't deceiving. The school had been closed for over a decade, when the town's population dwindled, and people there no longer had a need for it.

Like most old structures, the basement was a sound fallout shelter. Kevin told us he had been there for two weeks. It acted as a camouflage military base.

Two weeks.

That told me in the midst of the Youngen Virus, our leaders and miliary knew we were at war, and they braced for it.

Prepared for it.

The town had been hit by the Youngen Virus and the blackout, but those there were able to safeguard against the power losses and had a head's up on the incoming jets.

Still, despite all that, the town of fifteen hundred was down to a little over a hundred. Some had left town, some died, but there were many that arrived in small groups from outside of town; they were like us, refugees.

The town's folk and the military that were there had scavenged every home, store, and business for food. What we brought was a welcoming addition.

For the first few days we were all crammed in the basement until the radiation levels fell.

It was interesting to see Barron's readings compared to an official Geiger counter. Impressively, they were pretty close.

Even though we made it inside, my son Jake suffered from mild radiation sickness and was placed in the sick bay. The Army doctor said he'd get better, it wasn't a large dose, but enough to keep him down and out for a few weeks.

Weeks?

I hated to think how long it would've been if it wasn't mild.

He wasn't the only one. Several of our group were sick and showing symptoms within days of arriving.

Sam was completely gung-ho and watched everything the military did. I worked with Barron on that signal and songs in the former shop teacher's office. It was funny, no matter how many people we played that third song for, no one knew it.

There were these old-fashioned loudspeakers in every room. Rusted, brown box looking things from the fifties. They were even the rooms where people slept. Of course, classrooms had been converted into dorms.

General Collins, who had been a colonel before the war, utilized the loudspeakers often. Three tones precluded whatever he was going to say or an announcement by one of his staff. Sometimes I found it annoying, other times it was amusing. At least he kept things transparent.

"Ladies and gentlemen," General Collins spoke on the loudspeaker following those three tones. "It's now officially twenty-four hours since the last nuclear weapon detonated."

"Twenty-four hours," Barron said. "That's good news. Do you remember where they said it was?"

"Boise, I think."

Barron nodded. "We'll start to get a good idea on radiation now."

"How's it going?" I asked. "Any more letters?"

"No. But I know once I break and decipher one vowel, I'll crack this. That third song. What the heck is it?"

"You think it's really old?" I questioned. "Before our time?"

"No. Not at all. Even though it cuts in and out, it's not that old."

"Maybe it's an original," I guessed. "Like a band in their country wrote it."

"It's in English."

"Still, they've been crafty," I said. "I hate to say it. It's catchy."

152

"I'll give you that. It is catchy."

"It's so stupid," I said.

"What?" He chuckled. "The song?"

"No, this whole war and nuke thing. I hate it. Those weapons made no sense before and now it's even worse."

"We're alive. What makes no sense is how we weren't able to shoot them down. Did we not see them in the sky? Couldn't we scramble jets to shoot them? They came from our own soil."

"You heard what they said, they weren't able to. The signal was jammed or hacked."

Barron shook his head, shaking a pen. "You would think the top minds that remained would find a way to—" In his reach for a new pen he knocked over his cup. "Shit."

"Shit," I repeated, and as fast as he did, I started lifting things to get away from the spill. "Did it get your contraption?"

"I don't think I lost it, but I bumped it."

"Here." I was wearing an overshirt and took it off to get the spill. "You sure the coffee didn't get it?"

"No, I'm…" his words slowed down.

"What?"

"I found something else. Holy crap." He set it back down, then removed the headphones from the jack.

Immediately, I heard what he did as it played through his connected external speaker.

A foreign language. "Is that Chinese?"

"No," he replied. "Korean."

"How do you know?"

"I lived there as a kid for like two years. My parents moved around a lot."

"Are you sure?" I asked.

"I mean, I was like five, but still. I recognize it," he replied. "It's Korean. Can't make it all out. It's been a long time. It'll come to me." He listened intently. "Can you go get the General? This might be important. I don't want to step away."

"Absolutely."

I took another look at him while he plugged the headphone back in and reached again for his pen.

I hated talking to the General. I spoke to him twice. Something about the attitude of a man that promoted himself to the highest ranking official in the wake of tragedy.

As I searched out the General, I ran into Mr. Mosely coming out of sick bay.

"Everything okay?" I asked, fearful of why he was in there.

"Oh, yeah, it's fine. I was visiting Jake. He's doing so much better."

"Good."

"I mean he won't have all his strength back for a couple weeks, but he's a tough kid. Where are you headed, I thought you were working with Barron?"

"I am. I was. I'm finding the General," I said. "We picked up Korea."

<><><><>

General Collins was one of those men who dismissed things. I could tell he wanted to be the hero in all of it, hence why he was so gung-ho about giving Barron space to work. He heard the signal when Barron first pointed it out. He also didn't know the third song, but said the singer had a nice voice.

Yet, there he was, standing proudly, watching as Barron and another man, Dan, deciphered the messages. They shared that headphone set.

I was just as anxious to hear.

"It's more than one voice," Barron said. "They aren't sending a singular message. They're communicating back and forth."

Dan wasn't a soldier, he worked in town at a hardware store. Like Barron, he wasn't Korean, but he lived there. Longer than Barron, because his parents were stationed there.

Both though, were under twelve when they left. But together they were two halves making a whole.

"They definitely think they have an undiscovered channel," Dan said. "They hear the music, but aren't picking up the hidden signal."

"At least there's not mention of it," Barron added. "And they don't know the third song either. They think it's British, at least one guy said."

"What are they discussing?" the General asked.

"How hard they've been hit. No mention of nukes though. Just ground and airstrikes. They're saying it isn't China or Russia. Not sure where they came to that conclusion," Barron explained.

"Can you reach out to them?" General Collins asked.

Barron shook his head. "Not with this. I would need a transceiver, which I haven't worked on."

"Can you tweak one of our radios?" General Collins questioned.

"Sure. It could take an hour or so to retrofit it. Then the problem is, Dan and I have to figure out or remember the language enough to reach out."

"We can," Dan said. "I can work on that while he tweaks the upstairs stuff."

"Good. Let's get—"

"Wait." Barron lifted his hand. "They shot one down. They're like celebrating."

"One of those planes?" General Collins asked.

"That's what they're saying," Barron replied.

"They just said seven more to go," added Dan.

"They fly in groups of eight," said General Collins. "They cannot be all they have over that country. Or ours."

Barron asked, "NORAD can't see how many? I mean if they are attacking, they're refueling somewhere and stopping. Those ground troops are rolling in. They have to be coming from somewhere."

"NORAD can't see anything," General Collins said. "The hackers have control and radar. Like ours it's scrambled, and we can only get something when they're too close to launch a counterattack."

"Then hack the hackers," said Barron. "And unscramble the scramble."

"It's not that easy."

"No, it's not, but it can be done. I already did it. I found their hidden signal. That's on the same lines as hacking."

"I know you went to MIT," General Collins said. "What exactly did you focus on?"

"Building things, finding new ways to make computer science work for us."

Mr. Mosely chimed in. "In school he was voted most like to invent something to change the future."

"I could have," Barron said. "But family obligations called."

"Now your country calls. Do you think you can unscramble the radar or hack those hackers?" General Collins questioned.

"Well, I can't hack the hackers if I'm not in front of the system they are hacking."

General Collins nodded. "Understood, you'd have to be at NORAD."

"But I don't have to be at NORAD to unscramble a radar. You have one here, right?" Barron asked. "I can try. I'm like ninety-nine point three percent sure I can unscramble it. I unscrambled this signal."

"If you successfully unscramble our radar, I can pretty much almost guarantee they'll want you in NORAD. We're in contact with them."

"Okay," Barron nodded. "Give me a few minutes to get Dan situated and I'll be up."

"Thank you, son." General Collins shook Barron's hand and walked out.

"Wow," I said. "NORAD. That's where the president is, I bet."

"Safest place to be in that mountain." Barron gathered his things. "I'll tell you this." He walked closer to me. "If I go to NORAD, I only go if you, Mr. Mosely, and the kids come along."

"Barron, that may not happen. You may not have a choice."

"Then they don't get me." Barron shrugged. "It is the safest place to be. I'm not leaving you behind. Besides, they'll agree once they know I can do it."

"Can you?" I asked.

"Almost a hundred percent. And yeah, almost forgot. We'll need Ray too."

"Who?" I asked.

Mr. Mosely grunted. "The firefighter."

"Oh, that's right."

From the radio set up, Dan looked over. "What about me?"

"They're gonna need you here," Barron said. "But hey, if they don't, come along. Maybe someone there knows that catchy third tune."

"You're awfully confident," Mr. Mosely said.

"You know, usually I'm not," replied Barron. "But this." He pointed to his contraption. "Was far easier than it should have been. Like..." he stopped talking.

"Like?" Mr. Mosely asked.

"Every hacker, every inventor, every scientist, has their way of doing things," Barron said. "A method, a signature way. Like chefs had a way of making things. One may poach an egg in boiling water, the other may remove the pan from the stove."

Mr. Mosely tossed up his hands. "Where are you going with this?"

"The method is familiar," Barron replied. "I'm starting to wonder if maybe I don't know them."

"From MIT?"

"Possibly. More than likely a professor. Not saying they turned Benedict Arnold, but their tech could have been stolen.

Whatever the case, I'm grasping it easier than I should. Which tells me it might be something I was taught."

"Well, let's put that education to use...again." Mr. Mosely patted Barron in the back. "Not that I don't appreciate this place, but a ticket to Cheyenne would be very nice."

EIGHTEEN
WHIZ KID

Barron told me it was going to be at least an hour, so I took my notebooks and went to visit my son.

Mr. Mosely wanted a front row seat to whatever it was Barron was doing, but I wanted to stay out of his way. Besides, I had been watching him work for days.

It got a little tedious.

To my surprise and happiness, Sam was there. Since arriving at the high school and coming out of the basement, Sam was consumed by the thought of being part of whatever the military was doing.

He was standing by Jake's bed when I walked in. It was a large classroom, possibly the science lab. Jake was one of a dozen people there all suffering from the same thing,

With an IV in his arm, my son's bed was reclined to a sitting position and I heard them laughing.

Music to my ears.

"Hey," I said, approaching. "That laughter is good news."

Sam turned with a smile on his face. "I was telling him what Mr. Mosely told me."

"Which is?"

"If Barron figures out the radar we may go to NORAD."

"We may," I said. "I feel bad. I mean, we came here with a bunch of people from town."

"Yeah, but they'll be fine here," Sam said. "Mom, they are really confident in what Barron can do."

"How do you know?" I asked.

"They're positioning anti-aircraft artillery on the roof."

I whistled as I stepped toward the bed, and kissed Jake. He was pale, and there was some odd bruising on his forehead and chin. I didn't understand how my son was even affected when we weren't.

I tried to focus on him but I felt nervous for Barron. A lot was riding on his shoulders and he didn't even realize it.

"How are you?" I asked Jake.

"I feel better," Jake replied. "The headache isn't as bad and I don't want to throw up."

"That's good." I ran my hand over his head. "Did you eat anything?"

"Water. Soup," Jake answered. "Breakfast hasn't come up or out."

"That's good news," I said.

"That's *gross* news," Sam added.

"Are we really going to go to where the president is?" Jake asked.

I shrugged. "I don't know. I mean, we don't know if he's there. He's been broadcasting from somewhere right. And we don't even know if we can go. Barron has to fix the radar. And in my opinion, he's gonna have to knock it out of the park for them to invite him to work on the systems in NORAD."

"Can he?" Jake asked.

"I hope. He did find the hidden signal."

"A lot of good that does," said Sam. "We don't know what it is."

"The songs," I said. "I know the songs have something to do with it. He's figured out nine letters so far. No vowels."

"He needs a vowel," Sam said.

"Yeah, he has to have a vowel," Jake agreed.

"I know. I hate that his focus is gonna shift from the hidden signal to radar. He was making progress," I told them.

Sam asked. "Will we need it, if he can crack the radar?'

"Yes," I nodded "I think that signal tells us what they're doing."

"No offense, Mom," said Sam. "But why would the enemy tell us what they're doing?"

Jake guessed. "To stop them."

I pointed at Jake. "That's what we think. Someone doesn't want it to happen. Maybe they're trying to help us."

Jake shook his head. "In every movie, every book, there's always earthlings helping the aliens. Maybe one of them is a double agent."

"Can I tell you something?" I spoke softly. "I'm not discounting your alien theory anymore."

"A lot of the soldiers aren't," Sam said. "They won't say it out loud, but they said those jets are like nothing they've ever seen. Not to mention those suits they wear, Mom."

"It's farfetched, I know," I said. "But unless Russia developed some high-tech robotic suit, which they could have, we may be in for a surprise when we find out who our invaders are. They only thing that places doubt in my mind—"

Sam finished my sentence. "No mothership?"

"Um, what?" I asked.

"Mothership," Sam explained. "We haven't seen a mothership. Eight jets at a time are coming from somewhere."

"That's a good point, but I was going to say, the songs." I handed Jake the open notebook. "Hey, you guys are young. Look at these words to this song. Do you recognize it?"

Jake shifted his eyes over the words. "No."

Sam looked. "I don't recognize the words. You'd think I would, considering they're all the same."

"I know. Well, just think about it. Maybe come down and take a listen," I suggested.

Sam nodded. "We will. Is it catchy? It looks like it would be catchy."

"It is," I told him, then leaned down and kissed Jake. "I'm going to the ration hall, maybe get some food them check on Barron's progress. Did you eat Sam?"

"I did. Keep us posted," Sam told me.

"I will." I started to leave.

"Mom?" Sam called out.

"Yeah?"

"I would love to meet the president."

"Yeah." I smiled peacefully. "Me too."

My boys were well, mentally and almost physically. The one thing that truly concerned me was they rarely talked about their father or Luke.

I wondered, because of all that was happening, if they were putting up a wall.

The school was three stories, while some would consider it four. Built on a hill, from a front view the floors were completely above ground, the first floor was partially below ground level, and below that was a basement. From behind I could see all the floors.

The sick bay and ration hall were on the lowest level above the basement. Shielded some for protection by dirt.

I expected to be that person walking into an empty ration hall. But so many worked in shifts, there was probably never a time it was empty.

A few people, including General Collins sitting alone, were there having a late breakfast or early lunch. At first, I thought, 'Damn it, why didn't I go get Mr. Mosely?' Then I did that, walking straight ahead, don't see anyone move to the food line.

They had noodle soup and crackers and canned fruit. The soup looked like it was the type that came from a can, but that was fine with me. All the food was good food and I was grateful to have it.

Trying to eye a table away from anyone, keeping my stare forward, I realized it was useless when I heard General Collins call for me.

"Shelby, hey, join me please."

After a beat, I turned and faced him, placing on my best fake smile. "Love to."

Love to?

What was I thinking?

I walked over to his table, setting down my tray. "Thanks for inviting me."

"Of course. I was waving to you."

I shook my head slightly. "I didn't see you. I'm sorry. Just left my son in sick bay."

"He's coming along." Collins buttered his cracker. He must have noticed me staring. "What? You've never had buttered crackers?"

"No, never even heard of it."

"You're missing out. Here." He handed me a cracker.

"No, I can't. It's yours."

"I insist."

It looked strange butter on a cracker, but since it was the general, I squeamishly obliged. To my surprise, after the first bite, I couldn't believe I'd never had them before.

"Good huh?" he asked.

"Yes, it is, thank you." I handed him one of my plain ones.

"So, Barron…"

"What about him?"

"He's a gem. A genius gem. I've been in touch with NORAD and already they want him there, before he even conquers the radar. They want to put him on a team that's been working nonstop on it. They had no idea he discovered that signal."

"He'll break that code," I said.

"I have no doubt. I agree with both of you that the songs have something to do with it. I just don't know what."

Tilting my head, I lifted my mug of soup. "Neither do I. We're working."

"The okay was given for you, your boys, John and the firefighter to head to Colorado. A transport will be here in three days."

"Does Barron know?"

"Not yet. I just found out," said General Collins. "To be honest, I'm trying to move everyone there. It would safer."

"Plus, the troops could all work together. Especially if you figure out where the enemy set up base."

"Agreed."

"If you go, would you still be a general?"

General Collins chuckled. "Yes, why would you say that?"

I shrugged. "I don't know. You were a colonel before it all started."

General Collins smiled. "And you think I made myself a General?"

I paused before I answered. "I kind of did."

"No. Not at all." He wiped off his hand, shaking his head. "About four days after being here, the Commanding Officer, a General had a heart attack and passed."

"I'm sorry."

"I was too; he was a good man. The President immediately promoted me via radio."

I immediately felt foolish for thinking that.

"Just so you know," he said. "You aren't the only one mentioned that. I take it you don't like buttered crackers?"

"I did. I didn't grab any butter."

"Here." He pushed the dish forward. "I have plenty."

"Thank you."

"I'm very sorry to hear about the loss of your son and husband. I don't believe I mentioned that."

Pausing in buttering my cracker, I glanced up. "Thank you. How about you, General?"

"David."

"Excuse me?"

"My name is David. You're a civilian, please call me David. And…" He exhaled. "Everyone." He paused. "My wife, two sons, grandbaby, my mother—everyone. My, my little Rosebud." He took on this 'deep in memory' look. "My oldest daughter. No so little anymore. I spoke to her before it happened. She said, 'Daddy, we're fine, do your job.'" He closed his mouth tightly then cleared his throat.

"I am so sorry, oh, really, I'm sorry."

"Me, too."

"Can I ask when?" I questioned.

"Two weeks ago. Kansas City. First bomb to be dropped from an aircraft. Wasn't a nuke, if it was, maybe they'd be alive. I hadn't moved them. They were supposed to come here, after I got things settled. But a hydrogen bomb."

"I never heard of it," I said.

"Thousand times worse than a nuclear weapon. The thing was, it was dropped. It was ours. They got a hold of it."

Folding my hands, I leaned onto the table. "Does it sound strange to you? We're using our own weapons against ourselves."

"It does." He nodded. "But radio talk in Korea suggests Russian weapons were hitting Russia."

"So, every country is using their own weapons on their own soil?"

General Collins nodded. "It wasn't an attack from somewhere else. Even something futuristic like a dome of protection above our atmosphere wouldn't have stopped it."

"So, the long-range missiles we had for Russia, ended up not having to go that long range?"

"Exactly." General Collins sat back, playing with the spoon in his remaining soup. "It's like something more than us. Someone out there has the technology to use technology against us. I've been running through my mind what that could be."

"Alien?"

General Collins nodded. "That too. Or maybe, just maybe this has been in the works a while. Like some sort of science fiction novel, a combined country coup."

I took a bite of my buttered cracker.

"You don't think that?" he asked.

"I just can't fathom how that can happen. To what end? What result? World domination?"

"Possibly," he said. "Take down all the top superpowers, leave us reliant. Dependent. It certainly isn't to take over our land, because dropping that H-bomb, that made Kansas City uninhabitable for hundreds of years. I think if we can figure out their end game, we can figure out the why."

"Maybe we don't have to. Maybe they told us."

"What do you mean?" he asked.

"The words to the one song. '*If the button is pushed, there's no running away. There'll be no one to save with the world in a grave,*'" I said. "Maybe their end game really is the end."

"While that is good, the songs can't be a message to us about what they're doing." He shook his head. "The songs aren't a cover up for the signal or they'd play more than three songs. The signal is their communication. The songs are the 'why' for us to know and stop them. I believe it."

"General Collins!" an excited young man raced into the ration hall. "Sorry to interrupt, sir, but Barron said he found it. He found the back door."

General Collins looked at his watch. "Amazing. So fast." And stood up.

Barron was working on radar, the jammed signal and if he said he found a back door, he found something.

Just as quickly as General Collins stood and raced from the ration hall, I did the same.

<><><><>

"What's going on?" I asked Mr. Mosely the second I entered the room.

"He unjammed it, found a back door in," Mr. Mosely said. "Unbelievable. Didn't take him long at all."

"I know. Is he sure?'

"He's confident."

General Collins, arms folded tight, stood directly behind Barron.

Barron sat at the old school radar.

"Looks the same," General Collins.

"Wait for it," Barron said. "It's calculating range and if anything is out there, we'll see it."

"How far?"

"Nothing like NORAD, but maybe a hundred twenty-five."

"That's farther than we had before," said Collins. "We've been jammed at ten miles, twenty tops."

"Because they don't want you to have time or warning," Barron said. "It's sweeping now."

"And you broke it? For sure?"

"Watch." Barron pointed.

Suddenly the old-fashioned target style radar flashed and switched. No longer was there a circle with a clockwise moving sweeping radar, but it looked different. A green screen with objects at the top.

"Looks like an air traffic controller screen," said Collins.

"That's what it was supposed to look like. That 1940's sub radar look was a hack. I broke it. Shit."

"What?" General Collins asked.

"There. There. Ten. We have incoming. Headed this way." Barron looked over his shoulder. "We don't know if we're the target."

"We can't take a chance. Where are they?"

"South bound. One hundred and twenty-two miles out and coming. Fifteen hundred knots."

"Jesus, nothing moves that fast. That gives us…"

"Nine minutes," Barron said.

General Collins gave a single, calm nod, then turned to another man in the room. "Sound the alarm."

NINETEEN
DIRECT HIT

The alarms blared in the form of a steady, annoying buzz through the old-fashioned loudspeakers.

Three buzzes, followed by instructions.

Buz. Buzz. Buzz.

"This is not a drill; all civilians are to immediately retreat to the basement level. This is not a drill."

Buzz. Buzz. Buzz.

"All essential personnel, man your station."

My first inkling wasn't to run to the basement. Nine minutes.

If Barron had enough time to wrap up his work to take it to the safety of the basement, I had time to find my children.

I raced down the hall with Mr. Mosely to the sick bay, when I did, they were already moving people out. My son was gone.

Jake was moved first.

At least that's what I thought. His bed was empty. Usually, there were only one or two medical personnel in there, but at that moment, it seemed everyone ran to the sick bay to help. People that weren't in uniform were helping the sick into wheelchairs, and some were just being moved on their beds.

One volunteer for every person.

"Where is my son?" I asked.

"Let's find out," said Mr. Mosely. He led the way into the sick bay, trying to get people's attention. "Excuse me." He'd stop someone. "Where did they take the boy that was here?"

"They're moving all patients to the end of the hall. Excuse me."

"Not the basement?" he asked, but his question went unanswered.

He tried someone else.

I was looking around.

The end of the hall, it wasn't even the basement. If we were hit by those jets, it wasn't safe.

It was pandemonium. People moving everywhere, orders being called over the speaker system, intermittently the buzzing.

I didn't know where to go or what to do. I knew one thing: I wasn't going anywhere until I knew my sons were safe.

"Mom!" Sam called my name.

Being bounced back and forth like a ping pong, I turned around to see my oldest enter the room.

"Mom." He rushed to me. "You have to get below in case they hit."

"Where is your brother?"

"Down the hall. Other end of the building. I took him. Last room. That's where they're taking all the sick. It's one of those rooms that are half underground, the windows are boarded and sandbags are outside."

I nodded. "Thanks." I grabbed his hand then turned. "Mr. Mosely, let's go."

His attention was caught and Mr. Mosely hurried over to me. "Did you find him?" he asked.

"He is down the hall."

"Then let's go."

"Show us, Sam," I said.

"Mom, I have to go."

"Sam."

"I have to go, I'll be fine." He darted a kiss to me. "I'll be fine. But I'm fighting, Mom."

"Sam, I swear to God. Don't do this. Come with me. Please."

"I have to."

I felt his fingers slip from mine and in the mass confusion of everyone moving in a million different directions, my son moved from me.

No.

This wasn't happening. What was he thinking? Didn't he realize I needed him to be safe? All of the sudden he was going to take arms and fight this unknown and powerful foe?

"Come on." Mr. Mosely grabbed my arm. "We have to hurry."

"But Sam."

"Sam will be fine. You can't change his mind, Shel. Let's go."

I wanted to scream. I was torn; try to find Sam and stop him, or go to Jake?

There was no way I was going to the basement, not with my son in a room on the first floor. I understood moving the patients to the basement was hard and they probably couldn't move them fast enough. I also held high hopes that the room they placed him in really was safe.

Sam wouldn't take him there if it wasn't.

My heart ached with worry and fear. Not for myself but for my children.

Feeling the pull of Mr. Mosely, I moved in a near catatonic state.

That buzzing alarm was so eerie.

There were three staircases, one on each end of the building and one of the middle.

We weren't going downstairs, we just needed to make it to the opposite end.

We moved with the flow of people toward the middle stairwell. Once there, I told Mr. Mosely, "Go. I'll find Jake."

"Are you nuts?" he replied. "Absolutely not. I go with you."

Holding on to me, he led like a snowplow because as soon as we moved past the middle staircase, we were moving against the flow.

People were pushing by us, shoving, telling us we were going the wrong way.

And then as we finally reached the end of the hall, the sirens and alarms stopped.

Mr. Mosely flung out his hand, stopping the door to Room 101 from closing.

"Hurry," the soldier said.

We slipped inside, he shut the door. The room was black. No light peeked through at all and it took a few second for my eyes to adjust.

There were sounds of people crying, sniffling and coughing.

I saw a dim beam of a flashlight moving about. I should have known it was Mr. Mosely.

"There. Over there," Mr. Mosely said, aiming the beam of the light.

By the boarded windows, in a wheelchair was my son.

"Thank you," I gushed to Mr. Mosely, then raced over to Jake.

"Mom?" he questioned.

"I'm here. I'm here with Mr. Mosely." I grabbed his hand.

It was quiet. Were we safe? Were the alarms for nothing. If they weren't, what about those patients in the sick bay that were still there when we left? They weren't behind us and they didn't make it into the room.

A few minutes had passed and I believed we reached the point where it was probably a false alarm.

It wasn't.

Sinking into that semi relaxed feeling, because we reacted prematurely and in a panic state, didn't last long because the sound of the first explosion rang out.

It was such a huge explosion; it shook the ground and debris fell from above us.

The explosions kept coming, they were intermittent with rapid gunfire and distant booms. A song and response of war.

I shielded my son with my body, holding him for dear life. Cradling him, knowing I had him, doing my best to keep him safe, while my soul screamed in fear for Sam.

I could feel Mr. Mosely doing the same for me that I was doing for Jake. Protecting me with his body.

I didn't know who was firing the guns, shooting the mortars, or dropping the bombs. I could only believe it was an exchange, a fight, unlike in Hawthorne, because we weren't caught unaware.

The battle engulfed my every sense. The dark room left everything to my imagination. Feeling the ground shake and the debris as it fell against my skin with every boom.

Hearing the whimpers, the bangs, and cracks, smelling the smoke and tasting the dust that landed on my lips.

The planes of the enemy made a distinctive sound. High whistling engines with a slight roar as they flew overheard. I didn't need to see them to know every time they made a pass.

They were almost predictable, loud, close, overhead, fading, then gone. A few seconds later they return.

Rat-a-tat-tat, rat-a-tat-tat

That sound came from the building, it had to be those anti-aircraft guns.

About the tenth pass I had it. Forty-three seconds. However, soon they stopped. A minute went by, I was still counting. No planes.

One final rat-a-tat-tat.

Ever so briefly I thought it was done.

It was quiet, then the gunfire erupted again.

"They're in," said Mr. Mosely softly. "We're engaging on the ground."

I wanted to scream. That meant my son was up there, fighting and out of my protective reach.

I clenched my jaw so tightly, I swore it was cracking.

Please let Sam be okay, please let him be okay.

There was scuffling and thumping above our heads, a gunshot here and there.

Someone in our little room screamed.

"Quiet," another hushed. "Shh."

Please let Sam be okay, please.

"Shel," Mr. Mosely whispered. "Stay back here."

I couldn't see him well enough to mouth any words to him. He placed that small flashlight on Jake's lap and when he started to walk away, I caught a glimpse of him pulling out his handgun.

All I kept doing was begging in my mind, the same thing over and over. A message to the universe, a prayer to God.

Watch over him, please. Let him be safe. Please.

Crack.

Boom!

The door, our only door, burst open. The daylight from the hallway created a silhouette effect for the one enemy soldier that stood in the doorway.

He was covered from head to toe in some sort of armor, including a helmet. It wasn't shiny, nor did it look metallic.

The soldier that was assigned to our room was on my right, and the light from the hall partially illuminated Mr. Mosely, who held his weapon outward, as if on a practice range.

It was the first time I had seen one; for a second, I was shocked. I didn't know if he was a robot or not because I hadn't really seen him move. The blue lights on his neck seemed so bright. They couldn't be part of a human, but as he raised his rifle, which looked so similar to the ones our soldiers had, he moved normally.

Our soldier on guard fired at him and the bullets seemed to bounce off what he was wearing, creating sparks when they landed, not even fazing the enemy.

The guard soldier kept firing, but Mr. Mosely didn't. It was like he was either scared or he didn't know what to do. Just aiming like a movie actor portraying a cop.

What was wrong with him? He forged forward and froze.

But I got it, I understood, I could barely move. All the planning, and believing in one's ability to stand up to the enemy was all well and fine until it was real.

The enemy was real and he aimed outward, as if looking for a target.

Taunting us with his weapon.

The second he first fired everything erupted, screams and cries.

I watched as he shot an older man and then I dove in front of my son, covering him completely with my body.

This was happening, it was really happening.

Another one of us went down, a woman. The guardsman kept firing but it didn't make a difference.

The enemy soldier kept coming, the bullets deflecting off of him.

Another shot from the enemy and the man next to me went down.

I experienced sheer terror. My blood pumped, adrenaline far over the top. It took everything I had to breathe. I was frozen there, blocking my son, my entire being was numb.

He wasn't firing randomly. It was selective. He moved as if he were invincible.

I believed he was.

A shot here, another there, then finally Mr. Mosely fired his weapon.

Apparently, it was the shot he was waiting for.

One shot, one perfectly aimed shot and I watched the blue light spark extinguish, then the soldier just dropped.

It was over, at least that situation.

Spinning around, I checked on Jake.

"Mom?" he said my name with question.

"Sweetheart, are you okay?"

"Yeah, yeah, I'm fine. Mom?"

"Huh?"

"Shelby." Mr. Mosely called my name, grabbing my arm and turning. "Sit down."

"What? Why?"

"Shelby," he spoke to me like I was a toddler. "Are you okay?"

"I'm fine. Why?"

His eyes cast downward. "You were shot."

Thinking it was nonsense and he had to be mistaken, I looked down, bringing my hand to my side where he was looking. I couldn't see anything, but the moment I touched my midsection, I felt the dampness and immediate pain.

"Shit," I said shocked, the pain suddenly hitting me. "How did I not know?"

I felt lightheaded, almost drunk, not in control of my body. My rubbery legs began to buckle. I didn't know if it was the wound or my shock, but I was going down.

I heard Jake yell my name as Mr. Mosely reached for me, and that was the last thing I remembered.

TWENTY
TAKEN

Beeping, commotion and talking. It woke me, and for a second, I forgot I was shot.

I felt a burning and pulling, and when I opened my eyes, I wasn't in the sick bay, but I was laying down, my back propped up slightly.

"Mom's awake," Jake called out.

I turned my head to the right to the direction his voice came from and my son was sitting there.

"Hey," I said.

"Hey," he replied. "You passed out."

"I realize that."

Mr. Mosely came over. "Shel, how are you feeling?"

"Honestly, not bad for being shot. I know I passed out. Was it from loss of blood?"

Mr. Mosely shook his head. "No. Not gonna demean your blood loss, but I think it was shock. You took a hit to the flank."

"Well, good thing I have some extra padding there," I said. "So, it was a flesh wound?"

"Yeah, it was. Thank God," Mr. Mosely said. "I saw you get hit and I was worried."

"Can you tell me what happened? How many people did we lose?"

Mr. Mosely patted me on my hand. "We can discuss that later."

"Oh my God," I hurriedly looked at Jake. "Sam died."

"No," Mr. Mosely replied. "No, he didn't. We lost six people downstairs. None from the basement and I believe the general said four casualties and nineteen wounded including you."

"How did he get in?" I asked.

"No one knows. But we got him."

"Is Sam one of the injured? Is that why he's not here?"

"Shel, a lot of things transpired in this attack," Mr. Mosely said. "I'm not gonna lie. We also learned a lot."

"Did you learn about that soldier? The one you shot? Was he a robot?"

"No, he was a man."

Jake added. "And he's not alien, at least they don't think."

"If he is, he looks a lot like a human," Mr. Mosely added. "But right now, Barron is working on it. He's with the body."

"Barron?" I questioned. "Why is Barron working on a body?"

"Like I said, there's a lot to take in."

"Tell me."

Mr. Mosely glanced over to Jake, and I knew at that second, it wasn't good.

It was infuriating that neither Mr. Mosely nor Jake would tell me anything. I had so many questions, especially about Sam.

Where was my son?

After coming to my senses, I noticed that we were in the ration hall. It had been made into a makeshift infirmary and General Collins wanted to be the one to talk to us all.

When I was twelve, I was running to the screen door of my home. Thinking I would open that door with one push in my momentum, but my hands went through the glass. I had to get stiches. I rememeberd the tightness, the pulling and slight ache.

That was what I experienced with the gun shot. I was very lucky, another inch or so it would have been a direct belly shot, and I would have been a goner.

I grew anxious about knowing nothing and the longer I waited the more I knew something was more than just wrong at the school, something was wrong with my son.

I couldn't handle it.

There was no way I could handle losing another child.

I understood it was war, but I lost enough. I was done.

Those of us who were strong enough were moved to a corner of the ration hall, where others waited.

Even those not injured.

It was then I realized that General Collins was informing as many people so he could at the same time.

"I realize this angers you," Mr. Mosely told me. "I don't know much more than you. I just know that General Collins wants to have all his facts together in case anyone has questions."

I accepted it, because I didn't have a choice.

It had only been a few hours since we went to that room at the end of the hall. It seemed so much longer.

The school which was always in order was now in disarray. Windows were shattered, the walls were riddled with bullet holes and some areas were burned.

Finally, General Collins stepped in, he carried a little notepad.

"Thank you all for your patience, I know you're frustrated and angry and I am going to try to give you the information I can. I ask that you hold questions until I am finished."

There were a lot of people in that corner, but not as many as we had living at the school. A lot weren't there.

"At zero-nine-forty-two, Barron Acker unlocked the radar system that had been ambushed. He did so, saving everyone that is here right now, and the countless others out there working to get us ready to move. As you know, we cannot sustain life here and are no longer safe. A transport will be arriving in six hours to take us to a safe location. All of us."

He said to hold all questions, yet I sat there already waiting to ask.

"Because Barron unlocked the radar, we were able to see the attack coming from above. We were ready. Yes, their technology is far superior than ours, but our will to fight was there. We engaged, and our anti-aircraft artillery took down one of the planes."

Hearing that shocked me, I wanted to cheer and scream.

"We are still trying to locate that plane," General Collins said. "But one of the occupants successfully ejected and made his way in. We owe gratitude to John Mosely for his expertise marksmanship in taking out the perpetrator. While the outfit the soldier wore was impenetrable, John recognized the weakness. That weakness is also a form of technology that Barron is working on now. As far as we know, he is human, though we don't where he came from. We don't understand that suit, and I am being told, it's complex."

The general flipped a page in his notebook. "The enemy is smart, technologically advanced, and they know us. We know this because we estimate four people that have lived here among us were actually part of the enemy army."

Now that caused murmurs and grumbles of questions from everyone around. I thought it was time to pause to ask questions.

General Collins held up his hand. "These four people were not part of the town; they were a group of survivors that made their way to us. These four people aided the enemy soldier in strategically targeting elderly victims. They are gone, and we are certain they took with them four of the five young males from here, between the ages of sixteen and eighteen. We followed, but they went west via aircraft."

Four out of five young men. Jake was one of the five, the only one remaining.

The question of what happened to Sam was answered. My son was gone. Taken by the enemy.

TWENTY-ONE
TECH BEYOND OUR REACH

I freaked.

At first, I was calm, because we were in that meeting, and then it hit me. Another child was gone. Another one of *my* children was gone.

What were we going to do? How were we going to get them back?

"There's a reason they took that age group," Mr. Mosely stated. "They didn't do it to kill them. They shot through people to get to the young. They knew Jake was in that room."

"I want my son back," I said.

"I know. But take comfort in knowing that they didn't take them to kill them."

"It doesn't help."

"I know."

Then, as if he was my personal punching bag waiting to be hit by my words, I seized my chance to grab General Collins before he left.

"What are we going to do about getting the boys back?" I wasted no time asking him.

"You want me to fluff your feathers or be straight forward?" General Collins asked.

"Be straight forward."

"I don't know. They flew off with them and we didn't have radar because of the attack."

"They took the Factory Three people by vehicle," I told him.

"I'm sorry, the what people?"

"Factory Three was a neighborhood in our town of Hawthorne, people there were killed and others taken."

General Collins nodded. "They took a lot of people; I just don't know why."

"Are we absolutely, positively sure, this isn't some alien race."

"No, we're not. But I am hoping Barron can give us insight. Come with me, please. He has something. Maybe it will be a clue as to what happened to your son and others."

"General Collins. You said there were four people that infiltrated us, worked with the enemy?"

"Yes." He nodded.

"Are there more?"

"We don't know. I do know this, when we get to NORAD, they'll be very cautious about things. Really vet people. But that's for later, right now, let's see Barron."

I walked with General Collins and Mr. Mosely to the basement room where Barron was working.

It was his original working office and on a floor that was untouched by our hit squad. Dan was in there, along with Ray. It was a tight squeeze, and General Collins closed the door.

The moment he saw me, Barron rushed my way. "I am so sorry they took Sam. We're gonna get him back." Barron placed his hands on my arms. "We are gonna go to NORAD. I will fix their tracking, we'll find where they are holding up, we get one of these soldiers alive, torture the hell out of him or her until they tell us where our people, your son are."

"Hey, hey, son," Mr. Mosely said. "That's a heck of an ambitious plan."

"It's the only way Mr. Mosely," Barron said. "We need to get one alive."

"How do we know they speak our language?" Mr. Mosely asked.

General Collins answered. "Oh, they speak our language, the four that infiltrated us, pretended to be locals and refugees, sounded as American as you and I."

Barron looked back at me. "And if NORAD doesn't help us, we'll do it ourselves. We don't need many to go with us because we only need to capture one."

Then Mr. Mosely asked, "You make it sound easy."

Barron nodded. "It is. We'll use their technology against them. I just need to figure out how, but I am confident we can."

"What did you find?" General Collins questioned. "Confidence like this is bred from knowledge."

"First." Barron held up a finger. "That soldier Mr. Mosely shot, he was human. From earth, who knows. But he was human. You know those blue lights on both sides of their neck?"

We all nodded as we listened.

"It's biotech." Barron walked over to the desk and lifted a large petri dish. When Mr. Mosely shot on, it wasn't shooting the light that cause the soldier's death, Mr. Mosely hit the small window of flesh that was exposed, because…" When he showed us the petri dish, the round object was inside of it. "This thing was part of the soldier. Embedded in him. It's a form of tech but it's also biological."

He opened the lid, then using large tweezers, lifted the round object no bigger than a quarter by the edges. It looked black.

"As you can see, it isn't illuminating," said Barron. "I thought about taking it apart. But watch." He walked closer to Dan. "May I?"

"Absolutely," Dan said.

Holding the object he brought it close to Dan's neck. At six inches, it lit up, then four tiny tentacles emerged, wriggling around.

"Holy shit," I gasped.

"Yeah." Barron pulled it back, the object went black, and the tentacles retracted. "But wait. Dan, may I again?"

"Yes, you may."

Again, he brought it to Dan. Only this time, he moved even closer. Perhaps two inches from Dan's neck, from the center of the tentacles came a tiny pointed object. Like a thick needle.

"And that," Barron said. "Is how it attaches. It's self-aware. It's biological and alive, activated by human body temperature, something, because when you pull it away." And he did. "It goes dark again. It wanted to go into Dan. Basically, it thrives in the human environment. I have no idea why two are needed, but maybe one does one thing, the other does another."

"Any guesses?" General Collins asked.

"Not really," Barron replied. "I mean it could control thoughts, it could be a way, if they aren't from this world, that they adapt to the environment. It embeds itself."

"Is it connected to a life support of the individual?" Mr. Mosely asked. "Does it control the subjects breathing? Is it in the blood? Can we create or find a virus that kills it?"

"That," Barron swung a point. "I don't know. Very *War of the Worlds* thinking Mr. Mosely. It's not connected to anything vital that I can tell. See, as I said, you shooting the blue thing didn't cause that soldier's death, because the bullet came in at a slight angle, hitting the object and landing in the carotid artery. That's what killed him."

General Collins asked. "So, the one object he hit is useless."

"Oh, yeah, squirmy alive things inside are dead. I'm gonna autopsy that one. Pulling that from his neck was easy," said Barron. "The other, not so much, it wanted to hold on with everything it had. Like pulling out a stubborn tick."

"Okay," General Collins said. "Back to what you said. How do you plan to use their tech against them?"

"These things are connected to the tissue in the neck," Barron replied. "If I can figure out how to charge them, how to send pain, it could be quite torturous. Or we capture one and pull the probes. They could be controlling the soldier and therefore, we have released him and he can tell us what we want to know. Then we don't know what they do."

"Is there a way to remotely find out?" General Collins asked.

"Yeah, put it in someone. It's only one so it may not tell us much. But putting it in someone and monitoring them is the only fast way."

"I'll do it," Ray said without hesitation. "Put it in me."

"Are you sure?" Barron asked.

"No," Mr. Mosely spoke up. "He may be, but I am not. I would say a healthy individual. Ray, you have that heart condition. I wouldn't do it."

Barron cringed. "Sorry, Ray, he's right. The individual should be healthy. I mean we can try if you really—"

This time I interrupted. "No. Don't try. With the exception of this flesh wound, I'm healthy. Put it in me."

"Shelby!" Mr. Mosely scolded. "What the hell is the matter with you, woman? You can't do this."

"I want to," I said. "Barron said it isn't connected to anything vital. Monitor me. I feel very strongly Mr. Mosely that it's not going to kill me, and there's any problems, take it out."

"What about Jake?" Mr. Mosely asked. "You are all he has."

"No, I'm not. He has Sam. And if this thing can tell me where my son is, then it's all worth it." I glanced at General Collins. "David?"

He looked shocked when I said his first name. "I'll agree, but we have a medical doctor present and the first sign of trouble, the first sign that your vitals are not where they should, we take it out."

"Are you sure?" Barron asked.

"Positive," I said. "Let's do this."

TWENTY-TWO
WHAT WE DON'T KNOW

Doctor Francesco wasn't some army doctor or military at all. He was a family practice physician from the town. A middle-aged man who voiced his concerns and objections as he placed monitors on me.

Head, heart, lungs, blood pressure.

We had returned to the sick bay, half of it was in disarray. Bullets strewn cots overturned. We were in the far corner where things were still semi in order.

I sat in a chair, back to the monitoring equipment.

Doctor Francesco was behind me.

Jake was in a wheelchair not far from me and Mr. Mosely stood by him.

I asked my son if he wanted me not to do it.

"I wish you wouldn't, but I understand why," Jake said., "It's pretty cool and brave mom."

Knowing he was there helped me.

Dan, our Korean linguist, was there, along with General Collins and Ray.

Ray was pretty upset about not getting to do it. He really wanted to, but reluctantly agreed and came along to watch.

"We'll remove it if there are any problems," Barron told me. "It might be a struggle, but I think once the light problem is removed from the skin, the tentacles will retract and pull from the body."

"Let's hope."

Doctor Francesco huffed. "Again, this is absurd. Need I remind you that you about to place a biological, potentially extraterrestrial thing into this woman? Have none of you seen the movie *Alien*?"

"I don't think it's extraterrestrial," Barron said.

"Then where did it come from?"

"We don't know," Barron said. "Shel, you ready?"

"I'm ready."

"Since this was pulled from the left side of the soldier's neck, I am going to place it in the left side of your neck." He lifted the object from the dish.

"Did you at least sterilize it?" Doctor Francesco asked.

"As best as I could," replied Barron. He brought the object closer. "I wish we could have given you more than a topical, but we can't take a chance."

"I understand."

"This may hurt."

"I'm ready."

Really, I wasn't.

"Your heart rate is going up," said Doctor Francesco. "It's not even in. Breathe."

What did he expect? Of course, my heart rate was going faster, I was nervous. Who wouldn't be?

At the point when Barron brought it close to my neck, I lost all sight of it in my peripheral vision. I could tell by the expression on General Collins and Mr. Mosely, that something was happening.

"Tentacles out."

"Oh, good lord," Doctor Francesco said. "I ask you again to stop."

"Probe has ejected," Barron announced.

I took a deep breath.

"Shit," Barron exclaimed.

"What?" I asked, then I felt it.

"It jumped for you," Barron answered.

At first it was a crawling feeling, tickling and moving on my neck. Like a bug finding its way, and when it did, I felt the searing sharp pain as what believed was the pointed probe, plunged into my flesh.

More than anything I wanted to scream, but I held it in.

"How bad?" Barron asked me.

"Bad."

"Want me to remove it?"

"No."

"Doctor?" Barron asked.

"Pulse is racing, blood pressure rising. Any higher, you have to remove."

The pain in my neck was reminiscent of stepping on nail. Burning, pounding, and then it subsided. A warmth swallowed the painful area and I could suddenly feel something moving under my skin.

"I feel them," I said. "It has to be the tentacles. They don't feel big. They're moving. Like a nerve twitching."

"Blood pressure normalizing, heart slowing down," Doctor Francesco announced.

"What are you feeling now?"

"Same, they're just…" The swarming, nerve jumping feeling was soon replaced with movement. I could feel tiny movements racing up my neck. "They're moving. They're moving," I said with rushed words. "Up. They're moving up."

"Vitals?" Barron asked.

"Stable and good."

I clutched the arms of the chair as I felt those things go from neck to my head. I panicked. "They're in my head. They're in my head."

"Are you sure?" Barron asked.

"I feel them, they're all moving on one side of my head, like searching. I feel them."

"Does it hurt?"

"No, but they're in my head," I said with even more concern.

Mr. Mosely shouted, "Get them out."

"Stop this," General Collins stated. "Stop this now."

"Mom?"

Barron aimed the tweezers for the probe.

"Stop." I reached up and grabbed his hand. "Oh my God."

"What?" Barron asked.

"Give me a second to think how describe this," I said.

How? How would I describe what suddenly happened? Visually it was easy, but the other things, maybe they were my imagination.

Suddenly my vision had an overlay, like a video game or something. Words. Diagrams.

"Shel?" Barron called my name.

"It's like my brain is now some sort of computer. I see." I turned my head to Dan.

A scanning light went over him and his imagine was then outlined in yellow.

"I just scanned Dan. It says his heart rate is seventy-six. Wait." Words appeared next to Dan's outline. "It's analyzing him. Male, Caucasian, approximately thirty to thirty-six years old. Weakness right leg from previous femur fracture. The probability of threat eight percent. Unarmed."

"Did it just really do that?" Barron asked. "What do you see?"

"Like a video game. Outlines and seems to scan each person."

"Try someone else," Barron suggested.

I then looked at Mr. Mosely. Same information for him as Dan, but then the probability flashed red. "High probability of threat. Wait." I read more words as they appeared. "He's armed and, holy cow, it's telling me how he will use the weapon. That he will engage if three minutes."

"No, I'm not," Mr. Mosely stated.

"There's words, like I'm wearing glasses, they're just—"

"Do you need an escape route?" the male voice said.

"Who said that?" I asked. "Was that Ray?"

"Who said what?" Barron asked.

"Who asked if needed an escape route?"

"None of us said anything," Barron replied. "Shit. It's talking to your head. Think yes, you need an escape route. See what happens."

195

So, I did. I thought: *yes, I need an escape route.*

"Proceed to scan the room."

"It's telling me to scan the room. I guess it means look around," I said. I slowly began to turn my head and when my eyes cast upon Jake, a loud alarm sound went off. I could only figure it was in my head, but it made me jump.

Jake was suddenly highlighted in blue and the words big and bright. *"Criteria met. Apprehend."*

I stood up.

"Shel?" Mr. Mosely called my name.

I turned toward Barron to tell him what I heard and the same thing happened with him.

Criteria met. Apprehend.

I gasped. "It's telling me to apprehend you and Jake. Now it's like I know how to leave the room. How to take out the general, Dan, Mr. Mosely, all this, like I'm some sort of super soldier."

Mr. Mosely reached for his weapon.

"Take it out," I said. "Do what you need to do. If you have enough."

"We have enough for now," Barron said, leading me to my seat.

When he touched me, I kept hearing the word 'apprehend' and out of my control, I grabbed hold of him, twisting his arm behind his back.

I knew what I was doing, I wanted to stop it but my body had a mind of its own.

No, those things had a mind.

"Take it out," I ordered as I quickly reached and grabbed Mr. Mosely gun. "I can't control this."

General Collins rushed over, grabbing on to my wrist.

I kept repeating to take it out, despite that I kept fighting them. I tried, I really tried to stop, but I couldn't.

"Hold her steady," said Doctor Francesco. "Hold her."

"We're trying," grunted General Collins.

Then I felt a pinch in my arm, following by a war sensation pulsing in my blood.

In a few seconds, it was lights out.

Thank God.

<><><><>

It was the second time that morning that I was out. Blackout. Passed out the first time, put out the second by a sedative. One that hit me so hard, I didn't wake up until the engine and whirling of the C-something whatever aircraft was in the sky.

I felt the bump of the rough air and I tried to sit up, but I was strapped down.

Jake appeared leaning over me. "You're okay. We took off."

I tried to reach for my neck, but couldn't. "Is it out?"

"Yeah, it was weird, Mom."

"Tell me about it."

"Let me see if they can let me unstrap you. You can sit with me."

"Thank you."

Jake kissed me on the cheek and walked off. I turned my head to the right, there were seats against the side of the plane. Three empty ones in my view. I couldn't see much. Turning my head in the other direction, there was a huge area with boxes. I couldn't see what was on the other side.

I didn't feel any IVs in me or monitors, just a strap against my chest and legs.

Maybe it was a good thing that I was sedated, because I probably would have thrown a fit to know I was leaving without Sam.

General Collins did say the plane that took Sam headed west, maybe we were headed in the right direction.

My head hurt, like a hangover headache. The engines of that plane were loud and didn't help, plus the ride was bumpy. I remembered almost everything. Everything I saw, felt and knew. How helpless I was to stop myself.

"How are you feeling?" Doctor Francesco asked. He kept holding on to the gurney, swaying with every bump.

"I have a headache."

"That's normal. How about the embedding site."

"I don't feel any pain, but my side hurts."

"Yes, well, you tore your sutures open."

I sighed out. "I'm sorry."

"Any residual effects that you know of?"

"No, I feel normal. In control."

"Good. I'll go get the general. But first let's get you unrestrained in a seat."

"Thank you."

He undid the restraints and helped me to sit up. I felt dizzy and he said that was from the sedative. After helping me down, he walked me over to the seat next to my son.

Jake handed me water.

"Thank you."

"Slowly," Doctor Francesco instructed. "Sips." He buckled my belt. "Glad you're okay, Shelby."

"I didn't die, did I?" I asked.

"No. But it was a struggle to get it out. Don't be surprised if you're a little sore."

After he walked off, I reached over and grabbed Jake's hand. "How are you feeling?"

"I'm okay. You?"

"I'm okay. Where's Mr. Mosely?"

"He's upfront with the General. That's his seat next to you," Jake replied. "It'll take a couple hours and then we'll be there."

"NORAD?"

"That mountain. Yeah."

"You have to tell me what happened."

Jake looked beyond me, as if checking to see if someone was coming. "They want to—how did they put it—brief you."

"Okay, they can. But at least tell me how bad it was to get it out of me."

Jake snorted a laugh.

"What?" I asked.

"It was bad. I mean like not bad in you almost died, like bad in it could have been in some movie."

I crinkled my brow. "What do you mean?"

"Those things. Those tiny little wiggling legs that were like an inch?"

"Yeah." I nodded.

"They were like six inches when Barron got it out. He kept pulling and pulling."

"They were in my brain."

"I know. Did they really say to get me?"

"Oh, yeah. It was like not to kill you, but capture you. You and Barron," I replied. "But I don't know why."

"You think that's what happened with Sam?" Jake asked.

"I do. Do you know what all they want to...brief me on?"

Jake shook his head. "No. I just heard the General say that Barron should brief everyone all at once on his findings. Like the higher ups at the mountain. They're probably gonna wanna ask you a lot of questions."

"I can imagine. But thinking about it, Barron may be right. We may need to get one."

"Maybe you should have apprehended me," Jake said. "Maybe that would have told you where to take me and how to find Sam."

"That's an amazing idea, but it wasn't letting me leave that room without killing people."

"Wait until you see General Collins' eye," Jake said.

"What do you mean?" I asked.

"You nailed him, Mom."

Immediately I looked down to my right hand, it looked fine, but when I looked at my left, I couldn't see any bruising. "Did I hit him that hard?"

"Yeah. He took the hit, barely flinched, but his eye is like Rocky."

I clenched and released my fingers in a fist. "I would think my hand would hurt."

"Oh, you hit him with Mr. Mosely's gun."

"I pistol whipped the general?" I gasped in shock, then sipped my water. "I feel bad. He's not mad, is he?"

"He was fine. I'm sure he's had worse." Jake flung out his hand. "What did it feel like?"

"Out of control. I don't remember hitting him though."

"That's crazy." Jake lowered his head. "And you didn't have any thoughts on where to take me?"

I shook my head. "No. Just apprehend and get out of there."

"Maybe you should have said you didn't need an escape route."

"Maybe. Hindsight is a beautiful thing." Again, I sipped my water. "I'll tell you, Jake. This is scary. There's an army out there with those probes or whatever in them. I only had one and I know what they did to me," I said. "I hate to think what two of them together means."

TWENTY-THREE
TUCKED IN

"It's a complex biological technology," Barron explained. "It works to create the ultimate soldier. Left brain and right brain."

He stood before a long meeting table. Other than me, Mr. Mosely and the general, there were four other military men and some senator.

No president, though I heard he was there. I found it odd, I would have thought he would have been there.

I didn't get to see much of where we were. When we landed, they made those of us not on stretchers wait behind, while the ill and injured were taken. We then loaded into trucks and headed to the mountain. I didn't think about how dangerous the flight was until after we landed.

We could have been shot from the sky.

However, we were safe.

Once we arrived and drove through the tunnel, we were separated. Jake was taken to medical, while others were taken to be interviewed and 'vetted', I suppose they had a way to look for infiltrators. But I went with Mr. Mosely, the General and Barron to the briefing.

"I'm sorry," I had told General Collins before we began. "I am really sorry for your eye."

He waved his hand in a 'don't worry' manner. "I've had worse."

"Um," I kept my voice low. "You think the president is okay? I mean, why isn't he here?"

"Don't know. I'm sure he's fine," General Collins replied.

"Have you seen him?"

"No. But I'm sure we'd know."

"I'm thinking the same thing," Mr. Mosely said in a whisper to me. "And by the way, in all my years no one has ever disarmed me."

A part of me felt embarrassed for how I behaved, but I had to keep reminding myself that it was all out of my control.

Barron explained to those in the room. "We had one probe. That's what I am calling it for simplicity and understanding. One. I retrieved from the deceased soldier's neck on the left side. Apparently, this works with the side of the brain they are placed." He pulled out notes. "When Mrs. Doyle volunteered, I placed the probe on her left side. Now I didn't implant it, I brought it close and the probe found its home. It took two minutes for the effect of the probe to take place. Mrs. Doyle exhibited extreme enhanced left-brain activity. Thinking, logic, facts, sequencing. All of which appeared to her visually like, as she described, a video game."

One of the military men raised his hand and looked at me. "Mrs. Doyle, by 'video game' do you mean everyone looked different?"

"No," I shook my head. "It was like a data screen. People were scanned, I could see that. Their bodies were outlined in this light and words appeared describing them. Like who they were, their age, if they were a threat."

"I may add," Barron said. "That she also was hearing whatever it was talking to her. Asking her if she needed to escape. I instructed her to communicate with it, asking for an escape route and it not only told her what to do, it made her do it."

"I wasn't in control," I added. "I knew I wanted to stop but I couldn't."

"Left brain, right brain," Barron explained. "I can only surmise that a soldier implanted with a probe on the left and right side is totally controlled. The right side controls emotion, feelings reasoning. And I think and believe that the right-side probe shuts down those feelings to fight it. As Mrs. Doyle had."

Another Military man asked, "So, we have super soldiers attacking us without thought or emotions?"

Barron nodded. "Yes. I believe both probes work together to make the soldier follow orders without question or emotion. These probes are biological. They're alive. They are some sort of artificial intelligence that becomes embedded. Then in turn control the host."

"As science fiction as this seems," another spoke up. "We're dealing with something far beyond our capabilities."

"We are," said Barron.

"How do we beat them?" the senator asked. "Their planes are faster and more advanced; they have these super soldiers."

"They're just men and women," said Barron. "Men and women like you and me implanted with these things. I believe if we can find a way to take down the probes, we can reason with them. They may not know why they are doing what they are doing. Or maybe they do and like Mrs. Doyle, they can't stop it. We stop the probe, we stop the soldier."

"We're forgetting one thing," Mr. Mosely spoke up. "Why are they here? Why are they attacking us and what do they want? They have a mission. Obviously because they are taking countless people. When Shelby was influenced by the probe, she was told to apprehend both Barron here and her teenage son. They met the criteria."

"Is the why more important than stopping them?" another asked.

"Yes," General Collins answered. "We have been shot at, hit with biological weapons, we have dropped our own nuclear arsenal on ourselves. What is next? What is the plan? Barron can conceivably find a way to take out the probes. But these folks have a mission. They fail, someone else will come in. We figure out the why, maybe we can head off the next wave. And there will be a next wave when we defeat this one. They have a purpose, they have a mission, what is it? I for one want to know why my family died."

"There's a lot more," Barron said. "A lot more. We have our radar jammed, our computers hacked. A hidden signal beneath three songs, one of which we don't know. Everything that they are doing is beyond what we know. But...it's in the realms of what we know. These soldiers have feelings, but the probes stop them. I think the songs and the signal are their way to get a message to us. My core belief is that some of them, or one of them is trying to tell us something. They know us, they've watched us. It's time to know them."

"What do you propose?" the Senator asked.

"Simple," Barron said. "Right now, we unjam the radar, find them, because they're close. We get one soldier, that's all we need, just one and we de-probe him. Start there. Have two working probes. We find out the reason for all this, we find out how to kill the probe, we can stop it."

The senator laughed in ridicule. "We've been here for weeks. We have tried to unjam the radar and get beyond the hacking of our system."

"I found the signal buried beneath songs. I unjammed the radar at the school. I can do this because I understand this. I don't expect you to understand, Senator," Barron said. "It may seem to be above us technologically, but it's really not. We can break this. These soldiers are humans, probe or not, they need to rest, they need to eat. They're doing it somewhere. We unjam the radar, we'll find them."

"What about these songs? The signal?" the senator asked. "Do we forget about them?"

Barron shook his head. "Absolutely not. We work on the radar to find them and the code. One of them will give us the answers. And we're close to cracking their version of Morse Code. We have nine constants now."

"He just needs a vowel," I said. "This code will crack open."

"Alright," the senator spoke up. "Here's what we'll do. The probes seem key, we have a couple of key scientists here, we'll get them on scanning that thing and learning more. Mr. Ackers, pass what you have for the code onto our team to start cracking, maybe they can find a vowel and I need you one hundred percent on the radar and computers." The senator gathered his papers and stood. "I'll check in with you. I need to report to the president."

I saw on Barron's face, the disappointment that he was not leading the investigation on the probe or the code, both things he was critical in learning. But I understood where the senator was going. All three things were important in their own right. Barron was working on all three. His divided attention wasn't working in his favor for speedy solutions.

In my view, Barron had the most important job.

Find the enemy.

Find my son.

TWENTY-FOUR
PROBLEM SOLVING 101

There was definitely better medical care at the mountain than we had at the school and I didn't fault Doctor Francesco for that, he did the best he could with what he had.

I was asked to hold off visiting Jake until evening, they needed to give him some treatment and get him situated. I took the time to learn the compound as best as I could with how limited I was on where I could go.

There were a lot of floors and I was limited to two of them, while awaiting clearance for a third. That would be where I was helping Dan and whoever else at the compound was working on the hidden signal and deciphering it. I was happy to be a part of it and couldn't wait.

Until then I learned all that I could.

Two floors both located in the same building.

It was like a city within a mountain.

Several buildings and structures each, walkways, motor vehicles but instead of a sky it was rock and catwalks.

The floor where our meeting was happened to be the same floor as the hospital and cafeteria. The floors above were residential floors. Our floor was set up like some sort dorm or even prison. A common room with vending machines, shared bath-rooms, but the sleeping quarters were private. One or two beds.

There were two beds in my room, I suppose they were thinking Jake would move in before long, and when I went to visit him, I believed that as well.

In the eight hours that we were there, Jake had improved remarkably. Even Doctor Francesco was impressed. He was working there and in his glory that he had access to so much more medicine.

Jake's color had improved, he didn't seem weak, and he was eating a sandwich when I came in.

It was a proper hospital setting, not a classroom converted to one.

He was in a real hospital bed in a room with three others.

Jake was covered by a blanket, the sheets looked crisp.

"Hey," I said and kissed him. "How are you feeling?"

"Honestly, stronger."

"Good"

"They've been pumping me with something."

"I know," I said. "They wouldn't let me visit you until you were done with some treatment."

"What did you do?" he asked.

"I wandered around."

"Did you eat? Check out their mess hall?'

"Not yet," I replied. "I will."

"The sandwich is good. It doesn't feel like rations. So, you just hung out?"

"We had a meeting when we first got here. Bottom line, Barron is to work only on the radar and computers."

"That's not a bad thing, Mom," Jake said. "If he's working on everything, he can solve nothing."

"You're right. Me, I'm supposed to go to a briefing and interview tomorrow at six a.m." I raised an eyebrow to convey my thoughts on such an early morning event. "To get my clearance to work with the team on that hidden signal and songs."

"That's good. You have a knack for that."

"You think?" I asked. "Why would you say that?"

"Because you solve those Wheel of Fortune puzzles way early."

"I didn't look at it like that. Maybe I should," I said. "I'm just glad Barron is working on the radar. We need to find their base."

"Do you think that's where they took Sam and the others."

"I do." I nodded. "The why is what is getting to me. Why did you and Barron both meet the criteria to take you."

"There's nine years between us."

"I know." I reached down and grabbed his hand.

"Hey, Mom," Jake said, his eyes staring at our joined fingers. "Why do you suppose they are focusing on the young? I mean, the Youngen Virus hit everyone under thirteen and now they are taking everyone fourteen to Barron's age."

I shrugged. "Maybe save the young for the future. Maybe that age group can learn and adapt easily. Kill everyone else. I don't know."

I watched my son yawn. "Are you tired?"

"Yeah, it just hit me."

"I'll let you rest." I leaned in and kissed him. "I think about what we talked about. You do it as well."

"Good luck with your clearances tomorrow," Jake said.

"I just want to get back to work on the signal and songs. Damn that third song."

"And try to find a vowel."

"I need to find a vowel." I stood. "I promise to be back as soon as I can and keep you updated."

"Thank you."

"I'll let you rest." I kissed my son again. "I love you very much."

"I love you too."

I gave him a smile and backed up.

"Mom? Wheel of Fortune."

"Okay," I chuckled. "But I don't think it works like that."

"You never know."

"You're right," I said passively, and waved before leaving the room.

I was beyond grateful Jake was getting the care he needed. I felt settled with him. But my soul cried out for Sam.

I couldn't lose him.

With the loss of Luke and Cal, I just couldn't lose Sam as well.

Searching deep in my soul, I felt we would find him. I felt he was fine, However I didn't feel settled with that, because I knew, deep in my bones, there was something else we hadn't learned about.

<><><><>

There was a song playing in the common area on our floor. It wasn't loud and it shouldn't have disturbed anyone. A woman played it. One song. She sat in a chair, wearing her robe, listening to the song, when it was finished, she started it again.

I knew why.

It moved her. It was a song about loss and saying goodbye, something we all could relate to, especially on our floor. All of us were thrown together by one common denominator. We all lost everything. Our homes, family members.

While the song probably brought a sense of comfort to her, it made me sad because of what it was about.

The woman just stared out with a far-off gaze. She was lost, hurting, as much of a victim of war as the ones we lost.

After changing into some comfortable clothes for bed, I made a cup of tea and sat in the chair in my little room. I found myself like that woman, staring off, thinking. Thinking about Luke and Cal, missing them so much that the hole in my heart was a constant reminder.

And Sam.

I felt inside of me he was alive, but what was he going through? Was he scared, wanting me? As a mother my need to protect him was great but I was frustrated because there was nothing I could do.

I also thought about surviving, because that was exactly what we were doing.

We didn't have a home or anything we had before. It was all gone. I was certain that out there in our country there were places untouched. Folks in those towns meeting up at the local bar, trying to figure out what was going on, hoping to have power or something on the radio.

A safe town. A place where no one died.

Then again, I would have through Hawthorne would have been one of those places.

I sipped my tea, staring from my cup back up to the wall behind my bed. I looked up when I heard the tap at my door and Mr. Mosely stood there.

"I'm not bothering you, am I?" he asked.

"No, not at all."

"Thought you might like a night cap." He showed me a flask.

"I have tea and I would love a night cap." I held my cup to him and he poured the brown liquid into my tea. "Thank you."

"Long day, huh?" Mr. Mosely pulled up a chair.

"Yes."

"How are you feeling?" he asked me.

"Better. My side is tight from the stiches, but I feel better. I want this day to end so tomorrow looks better."

"It will. One day closer to finding Sam."

"I hope."

"I checked in on Jake," he said. "The boy is looking good."

"I know. I'm so happy." Sighing out, I glanced down to my beverage before taking a drink. "Do you think it will ever get better?"

"What do you mean?" Mr. Mosely asked.

"Will it get better or is this as good as it gets? They've been battering us for six weeks, right? Kill our young, our power, bomb our cities, shoot up our towns, take select people. And you know I don't think there are that many of them."

"I agree. The Korean radio transmission suggests small brigades. I think that's why they used our own weapons against us because that was their only option with their limited manpower."

213

"At this point in time though, wouldn't they have said, we have you by the balls, this is who we are and what we want?" I questioned.

"You would think. But I promise you, we will turn this tide. Barron is determined to crack what they sealed up."

"If we win, what then? Everything is gone, we have wastelands now. Everything is destroyed."

"Not everything. We're still here and we're still fighting."

"That's true." I brought my cup to my lips and paused.

"What is it?" he asked.

"She stopped playing the song. The woman out there was playing the same song over and over."

"Yeah, I heard. Not a bad song. I heard it before. Maybe she just filled up."

I smiled gently. "What do you mean?"

"A song can give you something you need."

"Not that song." I chuckled sarcastically and soft. "That was a sad song. The words are so sad."

"Maybe it gives her hope. I remember when I needed to be motivated, I listened to one old song over and over until I felt motivated."

"What was the song?" I asked.

"Swinging on a Star."

"Wait. The…" I sang some words. "Would you like to swing on a star?"

"Carry moonbeams home in a jar. Yep." He nodded. "That one."

"How are those words motivational?"

"It's not always about the words. Sometimes it's just the theme of that song. The sad song that the woman out there played was about moving forward after a loss. My song was about hope. Sometimes you just have to look at the song as a whole"

I took a big drink of my spiked tea when I heard his words. Truly heard his words.

Sometimes you just have to look at the song as a whole.

I nearly choked on my beverage. "Oh, wow that might be it."

"What are you talking about."

"I have been laboring over those three songs and the lyrics, word by word like I am studying for a test, when maybe the message isn't in the words, but the meaning of the song as a whole. Which…" I stood and walked over to my nightstand. "The lyrics if you don't listen can be deceiving as to the meaning of the song." I pulled out a notebook. "Dan brought this for me."

"The words to the three songs?" Mr. Mosely asked.

"Yes. But thinking about it, what if it's the meaning. What if the theme of the song is the message."

"And the connection to the hidden signal?"

I shook my head. "I don't know. I still subscribe to the theory that the songs are a message and not a mask, because why would they use the same three songs?"

"While we're having our nightcap, tell me." Mr. Mosely said. "What's the theme or, say simple tag line of each song?"

"Well, the David Bowie song you would think is about, well, changes, but it's not. It's about even being young you can achieve against all odds."

Mr. Mosely looked taken aback by that. "Really? You get that from that song."

"I do. When you look at it as a whole."

"And the third song?"

"Perseverance. Never giving up."

"That's obvious," Mr. Mosely said.

He stood and paced some, obviously in thought. "So basically, the three songs represent doing what you want to do, doing the right thing no matter what the cost. Seems to me, that maybe the songs aren't a message but rather an anthem for our attackers."

"Looking at it that way, you're right," I said. "Just seems we're have no real direction with these songs or the signal."

"We know it's a Morse Code of some sort, right?"

"Right."

"How many letters are they at?"

"Nine consonants."

Mr. Mosely nodded. "They need a vowel."

"I vowel would break it all open."

Mr. Mosely chuckled. "Sounds like Wheel of Fortune."

"Only there's no way to buy a vowel."

"Tomorrow is another day." He held his flask to my cup in a cheers-moment. "Eventually we'll break it. We'll find Sam. Eventually, we'll win this war."

I smiled gently at him, tapping my mug to his flask, then following it with a sip. I wanted to believe his words, but it was hard, especially with my son gone and the cities around us in ruins. If we did somehow win the war, what did we win?

TWENTY-FIVE
TURNING POINT

"Shel," his whisper in the dark caused me to wake up and panic. "Shel."

I sat up in bed and the table lamp turned on.

Barron was in my room.

"What's wrong. Am I late for my clearances?"

"No, and nothing is wrong."

I tried to see the time on my watch but my eyes wouldn't focus.

"It's four."

"In the morning?" I asked.

"Yeah."

"I still have an hour to sleep. Why are you waking me up?" I questioned.

"Get dressed. Then we'll go and wake up John."

"Why? What's going on? Are you sure there's nothing wrong."

"Positive." Barron grinning. "I did it. I cracked it on all fronts."

At first, I thought the enthusiastic early morning wake up was about the songs and signal, then I realized Barron wasn't working on that.

He continued, "I have everyone coming to the control room. I wanted you and John to be there."

"And you did it?" I asked, swinging my legs over the bed.

"Yeah, I did. Successfully contacted Korea and they were able to have their defenses ready for the attack."

"You picked up the radar that far?" I was shocked.

"Shel, we're better than before. We're global. Get dressed. I'll wait outside with the dead woman."

"Okay." I nodded and stood. When Barron left the room what he said hit me. *The dead woman?*

I peeked outside my door before closing it to dress and I saw Barron standing by her. The woman that was listening to that song. She was still in her bathroom, in the chair, but this time her head was slumped to the side.

Was she really dead?

Had she died and I didn't notice? Was that why she didn't play that song again? She was still in the same position as the last I saw her. I felt bad. Maybe I should have said something, asked if she was alright. The song she listened to was so sad, if what she needed was death, it delivered.

I wondered if she died from a broken heart. I of all people understood how that was possible. Every time I stopped, woke up, my heart felt crushed. I had to give my soul CPR just to get out of bed.

A part of me felt as if I should have just gone out there with her and Barron. He stood by her, hands behind his back, looking left to right as if he were next to someone at a bus stop. Just as I started to walk out, I saw someone come in and Barron stepped back.

Apparently, he called for assistance.

How sad it was for that woman to die out there alone with only that one song.

How easy that could have been me.

Holding on to the fact that Barron had good news and a breakthrough, I closed my door and got dressed.

<><><><>

The woman's name was Marilee. She was forty-four years old and had lost her husband, two adult daughters and three grandchildren all in one fell swoop.

One day. One bomb in Detroit.

She travelled with a group of twelve right after and ten of them were killed in an attack.

With just one other woman, they made it to Kansas, where a brigade of American Soldiers stopped them from going any farther.

It was too dangerous; the area was contaminated.

Marilee made friends with this one lone survivor woman, and just before they were to leave for Cheyeene, the woman killed herself.

Marilee expressed over and over that she had no reason to live.

No wonder she died. I would want to die too. No will, no spirit, no strength. I got it. The only thing keeping me going was Jake and the fact that my son was out there somewhere.

I watched them cover her face, so much sadness, and she looked so much older. I felt a connection to this stranger, maybe because of the common heartache we shared.

They took her away, carrying her out respectfully on a stretcher, then Barron, Mr. Mosely and I headed over to another building.

I thought there was no way we were getting in. The building was the heart of NORAD, housing the control room. But they nodded to Barron and we walked right in.

It was everything I ever envisioned it would be or saw in a movie. A huge room, loads of monitors on counter style desks and one giant wall with a map.

A coffee station was set up, and I helped myself. Other than me and Mr. Mosely, Barron and Dan. There were two soldiers I didn't know.

General Collins was the next to come in. His eye looked worse than it did the day before.

"I'm sorry," I said as soon as I saw him. Trying to stay in his good graces, I fixed him a cup of coffee.

"It's fine. It really is. Makes me look tough." He pointed to it, accepted the coffee and looked at the map. "He cracked it."

"Fast, too," I said. "Makes me wonder if we should toss him on the songs and signals."

"I have no doubt that Barron will put his hands in that as well."

"Morning," announced Senator Mitchell as he walked. I didn't know his name before, but Barron had told. He was accompanied by another general and a part of me hoped the president would be there. But he wasn't.

I looked at General Collins. "Still no president."

"He's fine."

Senator Mitchel shook Barron's hand. "Mr. Akers. Our thanks and congratulations. The President is right now speaking to Korea on that counterattack they launched. Very successful."

"Thank you," Barron gave a single nod. "I would have called the meeting earlier but when Dan and I saw the jets in formation headed to a target in Korea. We had to move."

"Understood," said the Senator. "From what I gathered, they have a good idea where they are setting up base."

Another General in the room spoke up. "Is it working? The board looks blank."

"Oh, it's working," Barron explained. "Nothing is in the air. Nothing of ours, nothing of theirs. Which means they are on the ground. But the moment that take off..."

"We know where they are," said Senator Mitchell.

"Exactly," Barron replied. "Now the reason I called you all here is because it's imperative now that we find a way to take out the biological tech that is implanted in these soldiers. Even if we know where they are, yeah, we can launch an offensive attack, but our best bet is to remove their heart, which is the implant."

"*War of the Worlds* style," Mr. Mosely spoke up. "They are biological, there has to be a way to infect them. Outer space or inner space alien, that is what you need to do."

Almost sarcastically, scoffing maybe, the senator turned to Mr. Mosely. "And we're listening to you, why?"

I heard it in his tone, almost demeaning.

"Oh, no," I said. "You will not speak to him like that. This is John Mosely. Respect him. Because you're some senator, you think you can take that tone with him."

"Shelby," Mr. Mosely spoke softly. "I can defend myself, thank you."

In the same manner, the same tone, the senator looked at me. "And you are, again?"

"Shelby Doyle."

"I appreciate the sacrifice you made," said the Senator. "Being a human guinea pig. But let's not forget, I am second in command of this base and to follow the old school adult and child rules, you'll speak when spoken to."

A high pitch whistle caught everyone's attention.

It was Barron.

He paced over to the main control panel and leaned against it. "Yes, well, here's the deal," Barron said. "I spent all night not only finding a back door back into your radar, but also expanding the radar's perimeter. These people, Mr. Mosely and Mrs. Doyle, are part of my team. You speak to them with the same respect you show me. If you don't, well, I pack up my knowledge and my friends, and we go to one of the two places I know for a fact that haven't been touched or hit."

"Are you threatening me?" asked the Senator.

Without hesitation, Barron answered, "Yes."

"And you say you know two places that are absolutely safe?" the Senator asked.

"Oh, yeah, and I'll go there. Bulowville, Florida and Calico, California. Both a distance, but safe and unhit. It's like our enemy doesn't know about them."

"We need him," said one of the generals after looking at us. "Our apologies Mr. Akers."

"I don't need an apology," said Barron, stepping away from the control panel and pacing to the coffee stand. "I just want to make sure it doesn't happen again. I'm busting my ass here. And we really don't have time for this."

"Agreed," that same General said. "What are you proposing?"

"System is up and running," Barron replied, refreshing his coffee and grabbing a bagel. "Put Dan in charge with a staff to watch the sky. I go back to work on the signal with Shel Doyle."

General Collins addressed the group. "I think that that signal is there for us. Others may disagree, but I really do. If they are using biotechnology, why would they need to hide a signal under songs. They have other ways of communicating, this is basic. This is for us."

"Very well," said Senator Mitchell. "We'll monitor the skies, Mr. Akers you can go with Mrs. Doyle to the lab for the signal. Scouting troops are going out at zero six hundred hours to check and create a safe perimeter. I'd like the people to get out and get fresh air while the weather is nice."

"Survivor recess," I said. "How nice."

I was met with silence. No one but Barron thought it was clever or funny.

"Carry on," stated Senator Mitchell and without even touching the nice coffee station, he and the others left.

General Collins let out a long whistle. "That was interesting."

"To say the least." Mr. Mosely bounced a little from heel to toe. "Exactly, what do you need me to do? I can't work on the bio tech thing."

"No, I need you to stay here. Right in this room and take notes," Barron replied.

"On what?"

"On what's being said," Barron stated. "I can't be sure, but I'm, like, ninety percent positive, they found a way to hack a receiver in this room."

"A bug?" asked General Collins.

Barron nodded.

Mr. Mosely tossed up his hands. "Well, a lot of good that information is if they know we know."

"*If*...if they have us bugged," Barron said. "They don't know that we know."

"We've been standing here talking," Mr. Mosely retorted. "You mentioned the only two safe towns."

"Which don't really exist. They did. Not anymore. They're still on all maps but they are ghost towns."

With an 'ah,' General Collins nodded and crossed his arms. "If they are listening, they're heading there, or will be."

"It's a test. Exactly." Barron looked over to Dan. "Are we still good?"

"Yeah, but they may catch on," Dan replied.

Then Barron turned to the two other soldiers monitoring. "All good."

One nodded, the other gave a thumbs up.

"Give me two more minutes," Barron said.

Dan exhaled. "It's pushing it."

"I know." Barron took a swig of his coffee. "What you see on the big board isn't what Dan and the other two are monitoring. They are monitoring the actual system. If the enemy has us bugged somehow, then right now they are listening to dummy conversation about the sky playing on a loop. I set up a back door to the hack. A safeguard so the systems don't get hacked, and, as an added bonus, I created a false narrative for the enemy, so when they try their hacking, they'll think they succeeded. The only time the system was on was when I turned it back on to reset the loops. Which so happened to be when I mentioned the town."

I raised my hand. "Before you turn it back on, what made you suspicious?"

"Because only a fraction of the sky we couldn't get, I couldn't get Korea at all, and a part of China. No sooner did I break through…"

Mr. Mosely finished his sentence. "Korea was hit."

Barron nodded. "I don't think it was a coincidence. If they were listening all night, they know I was making headway. The bug, if there is one, or receiver is in the system in here. It has to be all aspects have been discussed in this room. Which is how they know where to hit and when. They were making plans to come and get us at the school, when *what* happened?"

I sighed out. "The school was hit."

Barron snapped his finger and pointed. "Bingo. When we turn it back on, our conversation in a few minutes will be how it's failing again."

"Speaking of which," Dan said. "We need to start it. Loop is on its third time through."

"You're right. We know what not to say, others don't. That's why Mr. Mosely, you'll be in here. Go on Dan, fire it back up." He took a bite of his bagel. "Oh." He chewed really fast and swallowed. "Let's go get you cleared Shel; we have to get on the other aspects."

225

I grabbed one of those bagels and headed up the small staircase back to the door. General Collins walked with me and opened up the door for me. He looked back at Barron.

"Tell me again how that genius was a grocery store manager?" General Collins asked. "That man seemed destined to make a huge difference in the world."

"He just did."

"Imagine what the world would never have known had this war not broken out."

"I believe he was destined for great things. He would have gotten there," I said. "Sooner or later Barron would have left the store and made history. Just now, it's a different history."

"Wouldn't know it to look at him. What a trip."

As soon as he said that, I watched Barron race up the stairs, stumbling up the steps, nearly falling and catching himself before he made it to the top. "Ready?"

"I am."

I didn't know what getting 'cleared' entailed, but I was ready. I wanted to check on Jake then get to work again on the signal and songs.

THIRD PHASE

TWENTY-SIX
BEHIND THE HAZEL EYES

The clearance check wasn't as bad as I envisioned, it was less vetting than it was registering my fingerprints, picture, and handwriting.

I was done within an hour, and was told I was free to be in fifty percent of all areas. I didn't know if that was good or bad.

With some time on my hands, I went to see my son. Jake was still sleeping. I left him a little note saying I would get him later to take out for survivor recess if he was feeling up to it.

That was my plan, until General Collins stopped me on the way to meet up with Barron to tell me that The President and Senator Mitchell wanted to move all those who fit the 'apprehend' criteria to a secure location in the complex.

Considering that what we knew of the criteria was ages fourteen through at least twenty-four, we were going to be locking away half the military population.

"That's what the president wants," General Collins said.

I scoffed. "It's just Mitchell. I'm not convinced the president is even here."

"He is."

"You saw him?"

"Shelby." He shook his head. "Anyhow, they have viable candidate to implant the probe."

I paused in walking. "They're going to try it again? That's dangerous."

"They believe they can do it without a danger to the others. Maybe get some information."

"What time?" I asked. "I would love to watch if they'll let me."

"I am sure you can, considering you were first subject and you actually may be needed," he said. "I can radio you."

"I appreciate it."

I headed to meet Barron in the lounge on the first floor of the building next to the medical one.

When he took me to the lab, as they called it, it was not what I expected. A huge room with a long table in the center and walls lined with work counters.

There were three men and a woman in there. One of the men was working on what looked like old transistor radios, while the others had on bulky headphones.

Words to the songs were on the wall, but the music didn't play.

"We only have so many headsets," Barron told me. "We share. However, Bill over there." He pointed to the man working on radios. "Is fixing old handhelds so you those of us who want to listen to the songs can when we aren't in here."

"Oh, that's good news. Especially for that third song," I said.

"Tell me about it. Anyhow, this…" He led me to the table. "Is what has been figured out so far." He lifted pages with letters on it, no words. "At first, we thought maybe it was international

Morse code, which is simpler, but it's not. It's a repeated signal, we know."

"Why if it repeats are we having a hard time?" I question.

"It's not that simple." The man sitting the table removed the headphones. "The first part is the answer key. I'm sure of it. If I am right, it only gives eighteen letters, not twenty-six."

I looked at Barron, "Why didn't you figure the key thing out?"

Barron tilted his head and looked at me. "Do you really think I didn't? But unlike this gentleman, Mike, I dismissed it when I realized it was or could be only eighteen letters. When you get to the words, it's also hard to tell what are words."

"He's right," said Mike. "We all hear different things."

"If that is an answer key," I said. "Then you finally have a vowel. You have an A. The first letter."

"If it's an A," Mike replied.

"Has to be an A. Have you figured out any other vowels?" I asked.

"It could be anything."

Barron added. "let's do this. Let's assume this first tone is an A, and go from there."

"But are these D's or T's?" asked Mike. "Not many letters are double."

"Unless," Barron said. "It's not one word, but two."

"Rework them both ways," I said, then asked to listen to the tones.

I had only listened to the songs thus far. I mean, I had heard the signal but never really listened to it and was glad I didn't.

It was confusing. I had wondered why they had so much trouble, but when I listened, I had a hard time distinguishing a word from a letter.

It wasn't beeps and clicks like Morse Code, it was tones. Short, high, low, long.

But one thing I didn't have a hard time with. The letters on the paper.

"How many sentences are there?" I asked.

"Looks like three," replied Barron.

It looked like a game of hangman. Then it hit me.

I grabbed a stack of white paper, a marker and I wrote down every letter they figured out and in the same order they had them on the paper, I hung them on the wall, including blank sheets of the letters they couldn't figure out. Under them all I wrote down the exact tone code for each letter.

When I did, I heard Jake's voice.

'Wheel of Fortune.'

"What are you doing?" Barron asked.

"You have the spacing wrong," I said, then moved the letters. Some of the words they had were three letters, some more, but it was wrong, it felt wrong.

One thing kept catching my eye.

They had the letter T, but it seemed four times, the T was followed by what they had as a K.

"What if this K is an H? And the T isn't the end of a word but the beginning. Like here." I questioned, then replaced all occurrences.

I stepped back and looked again.

"Then that would be an E," suggested Barron.

232

On the blank paper I wrote an E for each occurrence after the E.

Mike grabbed the marker and filled in.

"Which means, here, here and here would be Es because they are the same code sound."

Arms folded, putting myself in my best television mode of watching the show, Wheel of Fortune, I stepped back and looked after arranging a couple more things.

I started figuring it out.

Hidden.

Melody.

Tune.

It started coming together especially now that I had two vowels.

"I got it. The first two sentences," I said. "Play the tune. The reason hidden in the melody of them all." I sung out my arm. "Bam."

"Oh my God, that works," said Barron. "Play the tune. Meaning the songs. The reason hidden in the melody. So, we need to find a musician to figure out the musical connection."

"Exactly."

"What's this last sentence?" asked Barron.

"I don't know."

I glanced at the phrase. It wasn't long. I added the letters to the mapped-out tones.

RA_NING _E_O_E THE DUSTING.

"Raining before the dusting?" I guessed. "Beloved is another, but raining makes sense."

"Wow," Mike said. "You must have watched a lot of *Wheel of Fortune.*"

"I did." I nodded. "My husband used to get…" I heard the static from my radio and lifted it. "General?"

"Yeah, if you can come to the biological lab, we're waiting on you."

"I'm on my way," I said. "Barron, locate a musician, I'm headed up to the other lab."

"Biological lab. Did they find a candidate to implant again?"

"They did."

"This will be good. I'm going. Mike…" Barron looked down. "On it. Musicians."

"Let's go," Barron instructed, placing his hand on my back as we headed out. "And good job solving the puzzle."

"Too bad I don't get a prize," I said as we walked out. "What kind of candidate do you suppose they found to implant?"

"I don't know, but I'd guess it has to be good," Barron said.

Good? Good would have been the least of what I would have called the chosen subject. Sadistic was more like it. General Collins was there and was standing before a glass observation window when we arrived.

The subject was asleep on the table. Two doctors stood over him, one was Doctor Francesco watching the vitals and the other I guessed was the scientist doing the implant.

I could see Al was older, much older and if I wasn't mistaken, was missing a leg.

"Is this a joke?" I asked.

"Nope," replied General Collins.

"Won't it kill him?"

"It made your vitals stable, so we think it won't do damage."

"So, you picked him?" I questioned.

"Well," Barron said. "I don't see how he's a threat. Is that his walker?"

"It is," General Collins replied. "Look, we needed someone smart, someone that could replay the information, and some physically incapable of being a threat. We sedated him because you said it was painful. While he didn't mind, we thought sedating him was best. We have our subject. Al is it."

"Al?" I asked. "How old is Al?"

"Eighty-two," replied General Collins. "Smart as a whip, sharp too. History professor at Cal U. Retired. Before that he served his country for fifteen years. Was injured in an explosion in combat. Lost his leg and his right eye. He volunteered. We'll be bringing two soldiers in. One armed, one not. Both in that age range."

"Interesting." Barron stepped closer to the glass. "Age, physical limitations should make it easier to keep him in control, unlike Shel, who turned into Wonder Woman."

"This." General Collins nodded. "Will be interesting. How is the song and signal deciphering going."

"Brilliant," said Barron. "Using her best *Wheel of Fortune* skills, Shel, here solved the puzzle. We know what the repeated phrase is.'

"That's amazing," said General Collins. "What did it tell us?"

I answered, "That there's another puzzle. The music of the songs is the key and reason. Whatever that means."

"That doesn't make sense," said General Collins. "They buried a message beneath the songs to tell you the songs are the reason."

I nodded. "Melody, it said. So, music. We're looking for musicians. We're thinking chord pattern."

"Still, it doesn't make any sense," said the General.

"Neither does the last sentence she solved," Barron said.

"Which is?" General Collins asked.

Barron replied. "Raining before the dusting."

"What the hell?" General Collins produced a confused expression. "What does that mean."

I shrugged and lifted my hands.

"General," the voice came over the speakers. "We're ready."

General Collins lifted his radio. "You can go in now, gentlemen."

Two soldiers entered the room and stayed to the back. It was weird. I had this painful reminiscent of the procedure as I watched the doctor hold the probe over Al.

It seemed much more medical then experimental.

"It's in. Mrs. Doyle, how long did it take for you to feel its effects?"

"You can answer," said General Collins. "They hear you."

"Within a minute or two."

Doctor Francesco announced how Al's vitals were steady and strong and then Al just sat up.

He ejected forward to a sitting position.

"Holy shit," said Al. "I can see really good. There's a grid of some sort outlining the soldiers. They are posing a threat, it reads."

Al turned swinging his body, as if he were going to get off the bed.

One of the soldiers brought his walker forward for him.

"Okay, listen, back up. It's telling me to take your weapon, shoot both these doctors and..." Al grunted. "It's telling me to do it now."

Knowing Al had the physical limitations, I don't think anyone was worried. When he hopped off the table, I expected him to fall.

He didn't.

He lunged forward, grabbed his walker, swung it out striking the soldier so hard, the young man spun and dropped to the floor.

Moving on leg as if he had two, Al reached down for the soldier's weapon.

General Collins flew into the room, then Barron did as well.

"No, wait," I hollered.

Then Doctor Francesco and the other doctor grabbed for Al, and the other soldier moved in as well.

Was I witnessing some sort of action hero from a movie and not some eighty-year-old man? He was strong, he moved with agility. Spinning toward Doctor Francesco, he hit him with the revolver, shifted his stance, aimed and shot the other man.

I screamed.

Then like a football player, Doctor Francesco raced forward, shoulder first, tackling Al to the ground. General Collins and the other soldier dove for Al. Barron joined in trying to help. Disheveled and off balance, Doctor Francesco stood and looked around on the ground.

They were yelling.

"Hold him," General Collins ordered.

"I'm trying," said the soldier.

"He's eighty years old for crying out loud."

Then Doctor Francesco joined the pile up. Only I knew what he was doing. He found the sedative because in a few seconds, it was over.

While General Collins didn't have another black eye, there was blood. Once I knew it was safe, I ran into the room.

Doctor Francesco was administering aid to the man that was shot. Al was out and Barron was already on the ground pulling out the probe.

General Collins stood and checked on the downed young soldier that was hit with a walker.

Out of breath, Collins faced me. "We can't do this again. If it made an eighty-year-old man like this, I don't want to think about what we're up against. We need to figure out how to disarm this thing and we need to figure it out now."

I couldn't agree more. I was going to do my part, which wasn't very much. I had to find Mr. Mosely and tell him what happened.

When I did, that little lab room wasn't the only place all hell was breaking loose.

Not that I knew for sure, however when I got there, clearances or not, they weren't letting me in that room.

Something happened.

TWENTY-SEVEN
SURVIVOR RECESS

"I told you that you were good at *Wheel of Fortune*," Jake said. "Dad used to get so mad at you."

"Yeah, he did."

"Are you alright?" he asked. "Did something happen?"

I wanted to tell him what I saw, that one of the doctors was shot, thankfully, it wasn't bad. Let alone I my suspicious about something going on in the control room, but I didn't. I didn't want my son to worry.

"I'm fine."

"We'll find him, Mom, we will."

"I know."

We sat in the area of the medical center, where a few tables were set up. Like a recreation room. They were waiting on their lunch. I wanted him to go outside with me but his doctor didn't think it was good idea.

He looked at the puzzle message as I placed it down. The sheets of paper and codes. Both with the missing letters and one with it filled in. He kept going back and forth.

"What is it?" I asked.

"Are you sure this is right?"

"No, not really," I said. "What do you see?"

"Well, it's just...raining before the dusting doesn't make sense. And...well. Look at it. The first I in 'Raining' doesn't match any of the other I codes. And the R in 'before' is different than both R's in Raining and Reason. So, is the R wrong? I'm guessing the S may not be right either. Look. The dots and dashes don't match up."

I tilted my head. "You're right. I was just guessing, filling in the blanks. Just, what else could it be?"

"It's a good guess mom. You figured out the H and E. Either way, we know Melody is right, so it all has to do with the songs."

I sighed out. I thought I had it. I gathered the papers, but left them with Jake, hoping after his lunch he could work on it.

Me, I was going to go outside for the break, take advantage of it.

I stopped by the lab where Barron was and picked up one of the song players as he called it. A handheld radio looking thing that played the songs through a loop and transmitted them. I wanted to take it outside with me, walk and listen. I didn't have the heart, perhaps it was embarrassment, to tell him I was wrong about the message.

Correction, I was wrong about what the words were, the meaning was still the same.

The melody held the key.

On my way out, I was surprised to see Mr. Mosely. He was steadfast on staying in the main room, eavesdropping. But he had gone outside and was on his way in.

"Stay close," he said to me. "Don't wander too far off."

"What's going on?" I asked.

"Barron was right. There is a transceiver in that room somewhere. The enemy planes took off for those two spots he mentioned."

"If they took off, you guys know where they came from."

Mr. Mosely nodded.

"That's good news."

"It's really good news. Last I heard they were planning a counter offensive."

"Please tell me they didn't mention that in that room," I said.

"They didn't. But they're putting this together. I pushed for canceling this survivor recess, but it looks safe."

"You came out."

"I did. For air, I just have a feeling we may be inside a while."

"But we have to look for those they took," I said.

"All part of the plan. They're close, Shel, they're real close. I just wish I knew what they were up to."

"What do you mean?" I asked.

"I mean there has to be something big, right? They can't be done. We all talked about the end game, and we still haven't figured out what that is. What is their plan? What do they want? They haven't achieved it."

"The songs are the answer," I said. "Someone on their side is giving us a message through the songs."

"I heard you solved the message."

I lowered my head and didn't respond.

"You didn't solve the message?"

"I thought I did, but Jake picked up that maybe I was wrong. Maybe I got the letters wrong. But I don't know what other words it could be. If it's not reason, it's not raining."

241

"That makes no sense to me," he said.

"It's the R. He doesn't think it's right."

Mr. Mosely lay his hand on my shoulder. "You'll figure it out. You can only work with what they give you. Last I knew, you weren't the one figuring out what letters matched with the tones."

"No, I'm not, but still."

"Still nothing," he said. "It's a warning. We just need to figure out what the warning is."

"That's what I'm out here to do." I lifted the radio style contraption. "Listen to it and hope something clicks."

"I'm headed back into the eavesdropping and remember…"

"Not too far. Got it."

I gave my thumbs up and walked forward,

It was nice outside; the weather was perfect and the air was crisp. It was easy to forget about all that was happening.

Soldiers lined the long driveway and people just kind of moseyed along. Some sat in the grass, some stood. I knew I had to listen to the three songs and without headphones everyone would hear them. I wasn't sure what people knew, I just didn't want to be that crazy lady listening to the same three songs. Especially the third which no one knew.

I had no control over the songs, I couldn't stop them or rewind, I just had to listen or mute.

It was a makeshift player made out of an old handheld radio. But it worked, the songs played at a low volume. I felt useful while listening.

While doing so I thought about the movie *Close Encounters of the Third Kind* and how music was an answer in those films.

I moved a distance from everyone, walking and listening to the music, not paying attention to how far I wandered. I was hoping something in the melody would grab my attention, something that I missed.

Outside the main tunnel of the complex was a road, it went down the mountain. I kept walking, not noticing where I went and was sure if I was going too far, someone would have stopped me.

A good distance from the entrance, still not so far that I couldn't see the tunnel, I found a nice place to stop at a bend in the road. Faraway from everyone and able to listen to the music

The third and unknown song was chipper and upbeat. Not that it was that unknown now, I had listened to it so much it was familiar.

I sat on the grass on the bend of the road, the radio for music on the ground next to me, eyes closed, just listening.

It was just under eleven minutes to listen to all three songs.

I was on my third listen through, sitting in the grass off to the side of the road, trying my hardest to find some sort of connection, when I heard the alarms.

They reminded me of the ones at the school, buzzing.

Four buzzes, a pause then repeat. It startled me and I grabbed for the radio that was given to me for communication.

I turned and started to stand, realizing at that moment how far I was from everything. I couldn't see if people were running. I was too far away.

Why didn't I get a call? Was it for real?

I pressed the side button on the radio and spoke into it. "Mr. Mosely. Is this for real?"

Static.

"Mr. Mosely?"

There was static again, then his voice broke up. It was hard to understand with Eve of Destruction playing in the background. I turned around again to shut off the music and there he was.

Standing there.

Not moving.

The enemy soldier. He wore what I would call almost armor. It reminded me of a thinner, more flexible storm trooper outfit from Star Wars. Only it was charcoal gray and the helmet was thin, not as round, not as bubbly. It was the closest I had been to one. He held out his rifle style weapon squarely pointed at me and he seemed frozen.

Not moving. Not doing a thing.

Cautiously and slowly, I lifted the music player, stepping back.

"Mr. Mosely," I said into the radio. "One is right by me."

Static.

This time, Mr. Mosely came through a little. His words still broken up, but I could hear the urgency. No sooner did that happen, I heard what sounded like a propellor plane. It was in the distance. Using my thumb, I lowered the volume on my music player to hear. As soon as I stepped back, the enemy soldier moved.

"No, keep playing it," the male voice shouted, and before I knew it, I felt the bodily hit of another person, slam into me just as the sound of close gunfire rang out. I was startled, it happened so fast. I landed hard on the ground, and the player was pulled from my hand. Not my radio, the music player.

Within a split second, Eve of Destruction started to play again.

I was on my side, more so facing the grass. The weight of his body lifted and I turned. The pain in my stomach burned and I knew my sutures ripped open.

I was expecting to see one of our own or someone I knew.

He wasn't one of ours.

He was one of them.

I was dead. I knew it.

He was dressed in an armor uniform as well, only his was a deep blue color, with some sort of case strapped over his shoulder. He knelt on one knee holding the music player and looking at the sky.

"Damn it," he cursed. "Out of time. Out of time."

He reached for his waist and pulled out something. I thought it was a weapon, it wasn't. It looked like half of a baseball, shiny and black. He brought it to my face.

"Put this on," he said. "It's coming."

"No. Are you nuts?" I scooted back.

"Put it on. Trust me."

"What?! No! Why would I trust you?"

Before I could do anything, he reached out, cupped the back of my head, yanked me forward and put that contraption right to my face. It felt organic as it formed a seal around my nose and mouth.

"You'll be alright now. Breathe." He stood, looking up. When he did a single crop-dusting plane flew over and a tail of smoke followed it.

In a fast turn of his body, he dropped the music player, stepped to the frozen soldier, reached out both hands to his neck and with ease ripped out the blue probes from the enemy in gray.

Immediately the gray soldier, once frozen, stumbled some and looked at the other soldier. I could tell, even without seeing his face, he was confused.

"You're good. They're out. Let's get in," the enemy in blue said. Reaching down he grabbed my hand lifting me to the feet. "Don't be scared, I'm not the enemy." He paused. "Okay, I am but I'm not."

"Who are you?" I asked, then it hit me.

The enemy.

"Where is my son?!" I blasted. "Where did you take my son?!"

"I promise I'll explain it all. But first, we have to save your people." He reached down and swiped up the radio. After fumbling a second, he pressed the button. "Seal the doors. Activate artificial ventilation. Do it now. You have six minutes. They just dropped the Strychnine." He grabbed my arm, signaled the other enemy soldier and he rushed me back toward the tunnel.

As we moved closer, my radio hissed. "I repeat," came General Collins voice. "This is NORAD command. Who is this? Identify yourself."

He lifted the radio. "Captain Conrad Fields, United States Airforce…sir."

"So, you're one of ours?" General Collins asked.

After a beat and pause in movement, Conrad replied. "Not in the way you think."

TWENTY-EIGHT
WISE UP

There was no way into the complex. Ten feet into the tunnel the first blast door had dropped. It was evident as we made it to the entrance that the single crop-dusting plane delivered something powerful. Six bodies lay outside, but I didn't find them dead. I watched them die.

It was horrible and there was nothing I could do.

They convulsed violently, crying out in pain until they were too weak to make a sound. Finally, they died.

It angered me.

No, I was furious.

I kept my distance from the two enemy soldiers, Captain Conrad whatever and Soldier 72-something, something in gray.

Him, the soldier without a name, I actually felt bad for.

"What did I do?" he kept asking. "Please, what did I do?"

He sounded young.

I asked three more times where my son was and was ignored, so I stayed away.

That thing on my face was stuck and the one just kept telling me it would come off when the air was safe.

"Shel," Mr. Mosely called out on the radio. "Tell me you're alright."

"I am. They put some sort of mask or something on me," I replied. "It'll stay on until the air is safe."

"Are you alright otherwise?" he asked.

"Yeah. They're ignoring me. The one wants to talk to who is in charge."

"We'll be out to get you soon. I promise," Mr. Mosely said.

"Is Jake okay?" I asked.

"He's fine. Just hang tight."

Outside, sitting there, I didn't feel in danger, just upset. I thought about a lot of things, a tiny part of me worried that it was my last moments on earth. How I would never get to say one last goodbye to my sons, just like I didn't get to say one last goodbye to Luke.

I thought about all the people I got to meet in our journey to survive the invasion. The general, Dan, and Ray the Firefighter.

I wondered what happened to Doug, the man from Factory Three. Was he alive? Were the others from Hawthorne? What happened to them? Did the Dearling family make it out of town safely?

It was a new era. So many people had died, but there was no news, no communications no way of knowing. Unless I saw them, I would assume those I knew from my town didn't make it.

Much like I thought about the president.

I assumed they weren't removing their headgear for the same reason my mask was still on. I wanted answers and they wouldn't give them.

"They're not going to let you go in there," I said.

"I have this," Conrad replied, tapping his case.

"Oh, I'm sure they'll just take it."

"Ma'am, I'm sure you all want answers. I'll give them."

He seemed arrogant, like in his mind he was the answer and they were just going to let him waltz right in and tell them things.

Conrad stood straight, staring at the blast door, waiting for it to open as if waiting on a bus. His head turned toward me. "You're bleeding."

"Yeah, when you knocked me down, you ripped open my sutures from where…" I raised my voice. "One of you shot me."

He had a batman belt and he opened a compartment, pulling out what looked like a large. green magic marker. He crouched down, reaching for me.

"What are you doing?" I swatter his hand when he reached for my shirt.

"Sealing the wound."

"Don't touch me."

"Ma'am, stop," he said firmly, pushed my hand away and lifted my shirt.

My eyes gazed down, he held the pen like object near my sutures and it looked like he cleaned it, then flipped the pen and sprayed something on me, sealing the open part of my wound. He capped it, stopped and put it away.

"No need to thank me."

"Why would I thank you? For fixing something you people did? Bunch of traitors. I lost so much," I said. "I lost two sons and a husband. I hope you achieved what you wanted."

"If I did," Conrad said, "you wouldn't have lost two sons and a husband."

249

Something about the way he said it made my stomach do a nervous twitch. Waiting for the mouth and nose piece to fall off, I sunk into my own thoughts. Replaying what happened.

I was about to ask about the music, when it hit me.

My conversation with Mr. Mosely.

Maybe I got the letters wrong. But I don't know what other words it could be. If it's not reason, it's not raining.

It was the R's, if one was wrong, they were all wrong.

"*No, keep playing it.*" Conrad had said right before he tackled me.

Keep playing it? The music.

The second I asked myself why, I realized that Soldier Seven Something was frozen until the music stopped.

"*It's a warning. We just need to figure out what the warning is,*" Mr. Mosely said.

Warning.

Raining.

I confused the R and the I, just like Jake said. Which means we had the S incorrect as well.

The word wasn't 'raining' it was 'Warning.'

Warning before the dusting. While I didn't know what that meant, I realized what the other sentence was.

Not, *Play the tune. The reason hidden in the melody of them all.*

The R was wrong, it was a W.

And I understood that fully, especially after all that happened.

Play the tune. The Weapon hidden in the melody of them all.

The songs weren't a message, they were actually the answer to stopping it.

The songs were the weapon we desperately needed.

Upon my realization of that, I looked at Conrad and the other soldier slightly differently.

TWENTY-NINE
SUSPENSE IS KILLING ME

The thirty-four minutes outside with the two soldiers seemed like an eternity. When the door opened and the gate lifted, eight of our finest, led by General Collins, rushed out and tackled Conrada and the other guy.

"This is unnecessary," Conrad spoke hard. "I am unarmed and have valuable information."

"Are you all right?" General Collins asked me.

I nodded. "I am. The music," I spoke soft. "The songs are the weapon; they stop the implants."

"Are you sure?"

"I saw it myself."

"Shel," Mr. Mosely called my name and with Barron, they rushed my way.

Surprising me, Mr. Mosely embraced me.

"I'm fine. They have a lot of gadgets for being our men." I handed the mask to Barron. "Here's another for you to look at. It's a respirator. It saved my life from the death dust."

"Wow. Cool. Thanks." Barron lifted it. "I'll exam—"

I waited. He just froze. He was stuck in a stare at the mask he held in his hand.

"Barron?" Mr. Mosely called his name, then snapped his finger. "What's going on?"

"Um, nothing. Nothing." He lifted the mask. "Just mesmerized."

As I began to go inside, I watched General Collins remove the helmet from Conrad. He handed it to Barron, but I didn't look at the helmet.

I looked at him.

I don't know what I was expecting to see. Maybe some sort of monster or roughneck looking guy with long hair and scars, instead, Conrad was a clean-cut man in his forties. Short military style haircut, I certainly wasn't expecting him to be clean shaven.

Handcuffed, he looked at me as he walked by me, escorted by General Collins.

Clearances or not, under normal circumstances, I would not be invited to the interview with Conrad.

Doctors examined the other soldier and Conrad was brought into the meeting room. I was told they were waiting for me to get there after Doctor Francesco checked my sutures and he had no idea what was used to seal them back up.

I peeked in on my son, then made my way there. I was anxious, hoping he would give all the answers we needed like a Scooby Doo ending. Both Mr. Mosely and Doctor Francesco didn't think he would.

I didn't know, he seemed awfully eager to help. Then again, according to Mr. Mosely, it probably was a trick.

Barron looked nervous, pacing actually outside the meeting room door when I arrived.

"Are you waiting on me?" I asked.

"Yes," Barron replied.

"Is the president in there?"

"Not yet."

"He's not coming; I think he's dead."

"Me, too," Barron said. "Shel, listen, before you go in. I wanna talk to you. You have become my real, true friend in all this."

"Thank you, Barron."

"Can I tell you something?" he asked.

Before I could answer, Mr. Mosely walked by to enter the room. "If you're confessing your feelings, I'd advise not."

I raised my eyebrows at him. "We'll be right in." I faced Barron. "What's up?"

He took my arm and moved me away from the door. "You're the only person I really trust, because, you know, you and I have always had similar thoughts."

"Okay."

"I think. I think I am the reason for all this."

At first, I thought he was joking, and almost laughed, but I didn't. "Barron, there's no way."

"Shel, I'm telling you. I have something to do with it. Not knowingly."

"Alright, I'm listening."

"Everything was too easy for me, figuring things out. I'm smart, but it came too easy."

"You said that, like you saw it before," I said.

"Or maybe I created it." He folded his arms tight to his body and bit his nails.

"Did you?"

"Not that I know of." He shrugged.

"Maybe it was something you did in college and forgot. But still." I waved my hands. "How would you have caused this invasion? The attack. Maybe something you inadvertently created caused their ability, but it didn't cause the attack."

"Shel, it is a gnawing feeling in my gut. Plus. I think I might have proof."

"Proof?" I questioned. "What kind of proof?"

"That this is all me. This is going to sound unbelievable or maybe it's coincidental. But…" He reached for his back pocket.

Mr. Mosely looked out the door. "We're ready. Let's go."

"Show me later," I told Barron as I walked back to the meeting room.

"I may not need to."

"Glad you are well," Conrad spoke to me as I walked in and sat down.

"Don't." General Collins pointed at him. "Speak to anyone or say anything unless questioned."

There weren't many people in the room. Myself, the General, Senator, Mr. Mosely, Barron, and two security soldiers.

"You're wasting time. Precious time," Conrad said. "Where is my case? I brought the case. It has everything you need in there."

"For what?" General Collins asked.

"To stop this. It already is too far gone. Where is your president?"

I mumbled. "I was wondering that myself."

Mr. Mosely shot a glance at me.

"What?" I mouthed.

"You asked to speak to us," General Collins said. "Talk to me."

"Can I least speak to Colonel David Finch Collins. Is he here?" Conrad asked.

"I am General David Collins," he replied emphasizing on the 'General' part. "So, I knew you before my promotion."

"Sir, no. But that case will explain it all," Conrad said. "Please, get the case and the president."

"That's not going to happen," General Collins said. "Let's start by you explaining why you are saying you are a United States Airman."

"I am."

"No member of the United States armed forces would be part of such a vile attack. Unless you are telling me you aren't part of that attack."

"I am not."

"But you are dressed the same," General Collins said. "Wearing the same uniform."

"Actually, my uniform is Air Force."

"Do you fly those jets that have been hitting us?"

Conrad nodded. "I do. But I did not participate in any attack. I tried to stop it."

Unbelieving, General Collins paced. "Are you an active member right now?"

"You can say that."

"Who are you with? Which Air Command?"

Conrad exhaled.

"Oh, I'm sorry did that irritate you?"

"General, we are wasting time, sir. You are limited on time as to how much death you can stop. Every hour that passes more will die." Conrad said. "Please, I beg you get the case that I brought."

"You must understand I have a hard time believing you want to help us. We have been battered, beaten, all by your forces."

"I understand that. That is what you see, I am part but not part."

"That makes no sense to me." General Collins threw up his hands as he walked. "Not that I expected it, but to believed you? You're giving me nothing."

"Rosebud. Forty-Three North."

General Collins stopped cold. He looked over his shoulder to Conrad. "What did you say?"

"Rosebud. Forty-Three North," Conrad repeated. "That was your codeword back in the day, it remained your codeword. When someone knew it, they were friendly forces. I am friendly."

General Collins slammed his hands on the table. "Who are you?"

"I will tell you again. I know that Geneva Convention requires all prisoners to give up information that can allow their country to know their whereabouts. This is my country. I am here to protect it. It is my job and duty and I am failing unless you get me the case so I can prove it to you," Conrad said. "My name is Conrad Fields. Captain United States Air Force. I was stationed right here. Right here. I flew out of the former Peterson Air Force Base—"

"Former?" General Collins asked.

"Former. My date of birth is Seven, Twenty-five, Seventy-four."

General Collins chuckled in ridicule "Seventy-Four? You were born in seventy-four. Looking at you, you expect me to believe that."

"Yes." Conrad nodded. "I was. You can check my information, but you will not find any records of me."

"You're in the Air Force, stationed here, and I won't find any information about you?" General Collins interrogated.

"No, sir, you will not," Conrad answered. "Right now, you will not."

"Because you're lying?"

"No." Conrad shook his head. "Because as of right now, I haven't been born yet."

THIRTY
The Why

As if he witnessed the winning of a football game, Barron jumped for his seat. "Yes, I knew it. This." He tossed the mask that I had worn outside at Conrad. "The name. The name of this manufacturer has everything to do with this war, right?"

Conrad stared at the mask, then glanced up. "Yes."

General Collins who was still in a state of shell shock, spun to Barron. "What are you talking about."

"That mask," Barron said. "He says he's not born yet, which apparently means he's from the future."

"You cannot believe that," General Collins said.

Mr. Mosely interjected, "There is no way. None."

"Look at the mask," Barron insisted. "Look at the name."

Mr. Mosely was faster than us all, swiping it up and looking inside. "AAIT? Okay. What does that mean."

"Acker Artificial Intelligence Technology," Barron replied. "Acker me. That was the name of my fake company at MIT for a final."

Mr. Mosely scoffed. "It does not mean that."

"It does," Conrad said. "But it can't be you," he spoke to Barron. "You're not the Barron Acker that designed this. You can't be."

"Is it my son maybe?" Barron asked. "I mean I don't have one."

"Barron Asker only had daughters. But if you are Barron Acker, according to our information you're only supposed to be eleven years old."

General Collins chuckled. "I guess artificial intelligence isn't that intelligent."

Conrad shook his head. "How could it be so far off?"

"Depends on where you looked," said Barron. "I wasn't born in America. When I went to college they had the same problem."

"Hold it." I lifted my hand and spoke. "The Youngen Virus hit almost every child under thirteen, was it designed to kill Barron? Was that what your war is about?"

Conrad nodded. "Since there was no viable, direct DNA sample, it was designed to take out anyone in his age group. But he is not the only target. There are thirty-four men and women that was the cause and contributors to the fall of the future. They are all located globally and at this point in time they are all between the ages of two and twenty-one."

"You destroyed lives, homes, families because of thirty-five people?" I snapped.

"I didn't. I tried to stop it. This war has been in the planning process for ten years. The only way to do so was to come here, to this time. And stop as much as I could. But all of my team had been interned for the invasion, implanted with the device. That is why I got the melodies out, the songs are a way to disable to probe and remove it, freeing the soldiers from internment."

Mr. Mosely asked. "If you could disable them, why didn't you do it yourself?"

"Because my device was taken, when I was taken. Luckily, I was freed and that was when I able to use an old emergency broadcast station in Indiana to get the signal and code out to whoever could hear it," Conrad replied. "Well, it's not old to you. It was just built."

Barron asked. "How did you figure out how to hack the probes?"

"Because you always placed a safeguard," Conrad stated. "You developed the probe late in life for use on repeat offenders and violent criminals. The probe didn't work, no matter how hard you tried., but then things happened."

"Things?" Barron questioned.

"Hold on," General Collins spoke up. "I'm not a scientist but I love my science fiction. If time travel is real, you can't travel back in time to destroy the thing that made time travel possible. Like if HG Wells built a viable time machine, you can't use it to go back and kill HG Wells. It changes the traveler's future."

"First," Conrad said. "There is no future. None that you would want to live in. Second, it's not time travel, it's one trip, one way only. The probes will die on their own and the interned will return to normal and remain here. That was the plan. Third, Barron and the others had nothing to do with the creation of time travel."

Barron began to pace. "What do you mean there's no future that we want to live in. What happened that caused the urgency to come back and kill me? What did I do?"

"You and the others are responsible for pioneering artificial intelligence to the heights it achieved. Taking it from basic text and images to medicine, problem solving and the lengths it took space travel. It was as if you all had to outdo yourselves. There was a point when I was young that life was easy because of it, but it grew and finally the human mind was unable to make it better and it started recreating itself. Producing its own forms of artificial intelligence."

"Wow." Barron shook his head. "It was replicating itself. Sounds like a bad case of incestuous reproduction, it went bad."

Conrad nodded. "I once heard a general quote movies that predicted it. Mankind was no longer needed in the way we are now. You are either a soldier herding people or hiding in small mountain towns trying to figure out a way to defeat or destroy the artificial intelligence."

"If Barron had nothing to do with time travel," General Collins said. "Then artificial intelligence didn't?"

"No, the visitors knew a way to conform and bend."

Mr. Mosely tossed up his hands. "Oh, for the love of God. Aliens? Are you now saying aliens sent you here? Eventually, you'll see, this is a trap. He's stalling us. Playing us. Time traveling aliens."

"No, it's not," Conrad argued passionately. "I am being honest. I tried. Now the only way to stop it is here and now. Get your president. He'll believe me."

"He's dead," I said.

Barron, Mr. Mosely and General Collins all looked at me and said, "What?"

"I think he is. No one has seen him."

"Shelby," General Collins said. "I was with him this morning. I assure you he is alive." He faced Conrad. "How in the world did aliens get into this?"

"I know it sounds so farfetched to you," Conrad said. "NASA has been sending signals out for as long as anyone can remember, trying to reach intelligent life. The AI boosted, and in that signal. They came out of curiosity, to see what we have. But nothing was even remotely salvageable here for them. Our green planet was brown, oceans poisoned, and synthetic food for most of us. They could not beat the AI. So, they began the plan. They created a worm hole that bends time and transports back. They do this often because they go back in time on planets to a point where technology is primitive to their own and the inhabitants can't beat them. Thus, when they return in their own time, the planet is ready to take."

In his disbelieving manner, Mr. Mosely shook his head. "Why now? Why not bend time and send you back to 1950 or, heck, even farther?"

"Because they weren't trying to terraform and take our planet. They wanted to help us and the best way was to go back and wipe out the beginnings of it all. The thirty-five, particularly Barron Acker."

Barron asked. "What's the catch? What's in it for them? You said ten years in the planning. They obviously had something to do with the enhancement of the probes. Are they such nice visitors they're doing it all for humankind?"

263

Conrad shook his head with a chuckle. "They want colonies on Earth. My guess is to enslave man."

"Same thing as Artificial Intelligence," I said. "Only with a greener planet."

"I won't be around to see it."

General Collins ran his hand over his chin and sighed out. "It's a great story. Really hashed out. What about all the people you took?"

"They are safe from the dusting. They will be the sole survivors," Conrad said. "But it doesn't have to be that way. So many people are left in this world. Now if you just get the case, I will open it and prove so much. Please," he begged. "I know we are running out of time. If dusting happens, those here in this complex and those already secured will be the only ones remaining. There is no antidote, no cure, it's an alien virus that they use to wipe out all life on planets."

"If this is true," General Collins said, "how do we stop it?"

"The weapon. The music. Get the frequency containing the music to every country you can. That will stop the soldiers from following orders. The longer the probe is inside, the more they forget who they are. Kill the probe, free the soldiers, they'll stop. They will all be at base when the dusting happens."

"And the weapons? The dustings?" General Collins questioned. "How many planes will there be?"

"None," Conrad answered. "It's one weapon. It will be launched into the atmosphere and that is all it will take. All life, unprotected, outside will die."

"When?" Mr. Mosely asked. "When is this weapon supposed to be launched?"

"September fourth, zero-seven hundred hours."

"Jesus," Mr. Mosely gasped. "That's twenty-six hours. How the hell are we supposed to do this?"

Barron tossed out his hand. "The music part and signal are the easy part. We can get that to everyone. I am sure they all use radios at the base, right?"

Conrad nodded.

"Simple, I'll hack into it. I got our radar back. Do you have a radio?"

"It's in my case," Conrad answered.

"What about the bomb?" General Collins asked. "How do we stop it? Obviously, it's set to launch."

"It can be disarmed. The rocket. There's nothing I can do about the virus itself, but we can stop the rocket. I can do it," Conrad said. "Take me there."

Mr. Mosely pointed. "And there it is. The trap."

"Please stop," I said gently to Mr. Mosely. "I adore and respect you. You have to stop. I really believe he is telling the truth. He could have killed me. What does surrendering give him? Find his case, get the proof and stop this thing."

After a heavy exhale that I heard, Mr. Mosely looked at me with tightly closed lips. "I apologize. At this point, what do we have to lose?" He looked at Conrad. "How will we know it's disarmed? How will we know you did it?"

Conrad gave a slight shrug. "You have the radar here. If I fail, you'll see the launch. Seal all doors." He then turned his head to me. "Thank you for believing me."

"Yep." I sat back, closed my eyes and lifted my finger. "Just one more thing. Where is my son?"

THIRTY-ONE
THE HIVE

It was hard to believe what I was looking at. A six-inch hand-held device that Conrad controlled like a video game, moving the camera to scan around until I spotted him.

"Sam," I wept his name, running my finger over the screen. "How many people are in there?"

"Four hundred," he answered. "Most between the ages of fourteen and twenty-four. There are a few elders and teachers. Some security. But several of the soldiers in there I know. They are not interned. They know what's happening?"

"Does Sam?"

"He does. This facility is in Washington State. It was designed by the government to house a thousand people for five years. The supplies were rotated to be fresh; it has its only water system."

"It's a bunker."

"A bunker, but we call it a hive. It was reconditioned to lock down organically for five years. That is how long until the air is completely clear and ground is safe."

"Organically, you mean alien technology."

"Yes." Conrad nodded.

"If they bomb doesn't go off, if the dusting doesn't happen, it will open, right?"

"It is sealed."

"But it will open if the air is good."

Conrad didn't answer.

"How? How is that possible?" I asked, feeling so defeated. "How am not going to see my son for five years? There has to be a way."

"I think if anyone could try it would be Barron Acker. But know your son is safe. He is safe."

"Worst case, my son becomes a man and I have to wait to see him."

"No, Shelby, worst case is if I fail."

As soon as he said that, the door opened and General Collins stepped in. "We're ready for you Conrad."

When Conrad stood, I extended his video unit to him.

"No, hold it. Watch your son. Show your other son," Conrad said. "Then hopefully, Barron will get into my uniform and you can use that to watch when we go dismantle the weapon."

I thanked him, but I wasn't sure I wanted to watch such a tense moment as he and General Collins and others go for the weapon. Until then, I'd watch my son when I could.

I knew why General Collins was taking Conrad, they had to plan, get the signal ready, and let Barron know if he was hacking into the right frequency.

What a heavy thing for Barron to carry. All that happened, all that was lost was all because of something I was sure he was proud of at one point.

I promised myself I would remind him of the good he was doing now.

Jake was doing better and I asked—no—I begged the doctor to let him leave the medical facility. Surprisingly, they agreed, but I had to bring him back daily for an intravenous. Not a problem. I had nothing to do now. Puzzle solved.

Our room was small, but it was our room. It would either be our room for five years if they failed to dismantle the weapon, or we could go somewhere else.

I got him comfortable. One of the soldiers gave him a crew cut, buzzed his hair because it was falling out. Bruising appeared on his body, some of them looked as if they were finally getting better. It was going to be a long road of recovery for him.

I didn't want to say much about what all transpired. Not until I had him in our room, where I could shut the door and tell him in private.

My enthusiastic, *Star Wars* fan of a son was more in disbelief than Mr. Mosely. The same son that insisted early it was aliens, just suddenly changed his mind when faced with the realism. That was until I showed him Sam. Jake had the same look on his face as Mr. Mosely when he saw it.

"Five years, Mom?"

"Five years. Unless, you know, Barron figures something out."

"A lot of pressure on Barron."

"I know." I looked at the screen, Sam was sitting in a chair with a book. "Hey at least your bother is reading now."

Jake smiled, looking tired. "What's in the case?"

"This was. Documents. Other things that he is sharing with president."

"When do they go and dismantle it or whatever it is they're going to do?" Jake asked.

I looked at my watch. "Right now, they have twenty-three hours before it goes off. That's twenty-three hours for Barron to crack the signal, get the songs playing, and for them to get to the base where the weapon is located. Thank God, it's not far from here."

"That's a lot to do in twenty-three hours."

"It is."

"If they don't do it, they could be right there when it goes off," Jake said. "General Collins too."

"Yep. He wants to go. I wish he wouldn't. But..." I lifted my shoulders and hands. "What can we do?"

A knock at our door caught my attention, and after calling out 'come in' Mr. Mosely entered.

"Any news?" I asked immediately.

"No, still working. They located one of the thirty-five in Korean. A nineteen-year-old whiz kid. They have him working on it. Bet he's confused. Maybe not. Maybe like with Barron it will click to him. I'm not interrupting, am I?"

"No," I replied. "Pull up a chair. We're just talking."

"About the big news." He scooted a chair next to me. "How about that?" he tapped my leg. "Sorry we argued."

"You argued with Mr. Mosely?" Jake asked surprised.

"No, just voiced my opinion."

"I was being obstinate and annoying," said Mr. Mosely. "Just didn't want to believe it. And boy…" He whistled. "That case is something else."

"I haven't looked in it yet. Just this." I held up the device. "I will when I'm ready."

"Well, when we do this, that case will be public knowledge. Entertainment."

"Did Conrad say anything about the songs?" Jake asked. "Why those songs?"

Mr. Mosely looked at me and shook his head. "I didn't think to ask."

"Me either," I replied. "I just know that they are a safeguard."

"From what I gathered," Mr. Mosely said. "It's shuts down the Artificial Intelligence, which I guess shuts down that wiggly tentacle things." He moved his fingers around.

"I can't believe this," said Jake. "Future soldiers, our own attacking us using alien technology. All to give the planet to the aliens."

"Yeah, how about that," Mr. Mosely said. "Your mom filled you in really well."

"She did."

"But you know what, son? None of that matters. None of it. Not the alien technology, the future soldiers, the worm hold bending time machine thingy."

"How can you say that?" my son questioned.

"Because in less than a day, it all becomes fiction again. What matters is people, lives, how we preserver and how the human race survives it all. And you know what?" Mr. Mosely winked "We will."

<>< ><><>

I grew tired of waiting, not hearing anything, no updates, which to me didn't mean, no news is good news.

I asked Mr. Mosely and General Collins and neither of them had anything to tell me. Dinner came and went, I even dozed off, but as it crept into the evening, I had to find out myself. I didn't bother him, but the one person who would know was Barron and I sought him out.

Dan was there and all he said was, "We've done all we can do. Barron went back to his room for a little."

I didn't know what that meant. Did they fail? Did they succeed? I just saw General Collins and he didn't even look as if he were getting ready to go on a mission.

I needed to speak to Barron.

Barron didn't live with the rest of us in those small rooms. He had his own room not far from his working lab. It was much nicer and bigger than what we had and as I approached the door, I heard thumping. A little scared, I knocked.

"Who is it?" he asked.

"Shelby? Can I come in?"

"Yes. It's not locked."

I opened the door and when I stepped in, Barron was in the middle of his living room, holding a bottle and doing something I rarely saw him do—drinking.

He looked a little drunk.

"Are you all right?" I asked, closing the door.

"Nope."

My heart sunk. "Barron, no one expected you to solve every-thing. It's okay. You tried."

"What are you talking about?"

"You're drunk, or getting there. Something didn't work."

"Oh, the radio hacking? Done. We'll have a front seat to it all watching it on some little hand-held video player." He downed his drink. "Some smart kid in Russian, not Korea, I thought he would be it, but some sixteen-year-old Russian kid figured out their radio pieces. Bet he's the one that ended up starting this all, not me. Hey, who knows, maybe he can crack the five-year alien chamber thing."

"Are you mad?"

"No. I'm happy. We're ready. Hopefully, this Conrad soldier does what he says he can do and dismantles the weapon. We only have…" He squinted and looked at his watch. "Seven and a half hours, but what the heck, it's only a two-hour drive."

"Cutting it close."

"Very close." He lifted his empty glass and poured some more. "I'm sorry, did you want one?"

"No, I'm good."

"I'm going."

"Where?" I asked.

"Tomorrow or later. Oh, I better stop drinking." He finished the small drink and handed me the bottle. "Don't let me have that I have a few hours to sober up."

"Barron, it sounds like everything is in order, what is it? What's wrong? I asked if you were all right and you said no."

"A billion, Shel. A billion people dead, so many kids, your kid, died because of my ambition thirty years from now."

"There would be more if it wasn't for all you are doing now?"

"Why didn't I stay at the grocery store?"

"You wanted to change the world."

Barron laughed. "I did."

"Barron."

"According to Conrad, they thought I'd be dead. They brought the information for General—no, I'm sorry—*Colonel* Collins, as he said. My life. In that case, I saw what my life was. And it," he nodded as he plopped on his sofa. "Was a good life. You, took over the store."

"Me?'

"Oh, like you didn't that coming. The longest running employee. I sold it you, well technically to Mr. Mosely, but it was yours."

"Really?"

"Yes." He nodded. "I saw my life. My hair had some strange phases. I married late, like forty. Went on to have three beautiful daughters, a semi attractive wife." He tilted his head. "Maybe the picture was bad. All stuff I will never have."

"Yes, you will have that," I told him. "You will. Those girls are meant to be, you'll have them. Maybe not the same semi attractive wife." I laughed. "Is she really?"

Barron shook his head in an 'I don't know' manner.

"You need to sober up. I'll make you some coffee."

"Thank you."

I walked over to his little kitchen area. "You've done a lot of good. You can't be upset about things that haven't happened. Like visiting a fortune teller and hearing things. None of it happened. Okay?" I put the instant coffee in a cup and turned on the pot of water.

"Yes." He exhaled. "Will you marry me? I mean, when you're done mourning Cal and stuff?"

"No." I laughed. "I'm too old and can't give you those three girls."

"Go it."

"Listen. I know you're tired and a little sad, but when you're done saving the world tomorrow, I need you to focus on getting my son." I watched the steam rise in the water, and figuring it was hot enough, I poured it in the cup.

"I can try."

After stirring the coffee and adding creamer, I took it to him. "That's all I can ask."

He took the cup as I handed it to him. "You're a good friend, Shel."

"You are too." I sat down next to him. "Thank you for all you've done."

Barron sipped his coffee, recoiled at how hot it was and nodded.

"Did you find out why those three songs?"

"No." He replied, sounding almost angry at himself. "But I will. Especially that third song. What the heck is it?"

We laughed about it in the tense moments of the night before the big battle or bomb dismantling. With all that was going on, a little laughter didn't hurt. It was needed. Even though Conrad delivered my Scooby Doo reveal of answers, I still didn't know about those songs. Yes, they were weapons. But why them?

I was confident I would find out, just like I was confident one way or another, it was all going to be over in less than eight hours.

THIRTY-TWO
SAVE THE WORLD

The war room was off limits to me. That's what they were calling it: the war room. It was the room with the radar. Even though previously I had the clearances to go in there, I wasn't permitted this time.

Neither was Mr. Mosely.

The senator, other generals, soldiers, and I heard the President were all in there.

It was bothersome, but I understood. There was nothing we could do; we'd be in the way.

That handheld device wasn't the only one. It was the one Conrad gave me. Barron had adjusted and hacked into it, enabling me and Mr. Mosely to watch as it all unfolded.

We did so in the break room twenty feet down the hall from the command.

Just before dawn, I said goodbye to Barron and General Collins as their team headed out.

General Collins was outfitted in Soldier 72-Something's uniform. Which meant he had the camera in his helmet. We would watch from his and Conrad's point of view.

I connected the earphones, sharing them with Mr. Mosely. Their voices came through. Not Barron's or the other soldiers.

They said they were shutting it off until they arrived.

The screen was black for nearly two hours.

When it came back on, I could hear a hint of Eve of Destruction, the sour note sounding version that contained the weapon.

It played in the distance, picked up by the microphones in their suits.

It was hard to see what exactly was happening. The screen was split, one side from General Collins, the right from Conrad. Even though they didn't move fast, the cameras bounced causing me slight motion sickness.

"Does he know where to find it?" I asked Mr. Mosely.

"He said he was there when they fitted the rocket with the weapon."

"How does he know how to disarm it?"

"He needs to get to the launch room," said Mr. Mosely. "He said that the soldiers there should be without probes. As long as there's power, he can manually shut it from the controls."

"Okay," I replied. "What if there's no power?"

"Then he has to go into the silo. He's confident."

"We're going down to the wire, aren't we?"

"We're going down to the wire, yes."

In nail biting mode, I returned my attention to the screen, forcing myself to occasionally look away to stop the nausea.

Left to right, General Collins looked about. I could see the future soldiers, just standing there, frozen. "Looks like the weapon worked," said Collins.

"Barron removed the probes as you passed," directed Conrad. "Everyone pull out the probes from each soldier. Just in case."

"Which way?" General Collins asked.

"There." Conrad moved ahead. The split screen was even more confusing. On the right the building grew closer, on the left was Conrad ahead of Collins.

I looked away briefly.

"Are you all right?" Mr. Mosely asked.

"Just making me sick."

"Yeah, it's hard to watch. What the hell?" Mr. Mosely stood up. "What the hell is that?"

I looked at him before looking back down to the device, he looked startled and perplexed.

"There." He repeated with a point of his finger.

There was nothing on Conrad's side, but from General Collins' view I saw two things scurry fast across the rood of the building.

Conrad stopped moving. "It's them."

"Them?" General Collins asked.

"Assurance. I didn't know they came through," Conrad spoke rushed, then turned. "Pull back, stay hidden. Barron get to cover now."

"Can they be killed?" asked Collins.

"Easier than you and me in these suits."

"Let's take these bastards out."

"Careful, they're like cockroaches. Where there's one, there are many."

General Collins sounded authoritative as he called out, "Bently take a sniper position. Cross, to the left, Barron. Cover."

"This isn't going to work," I murmured. "They have very little time."

"They'll do it. I can't believe they're here," Mr. Mosely said.

I glanced at my watch. How did time fly by so fast. They had seventeen minutes.

It was crazy watching it, left and right they moved their heads. Conrad was ahead of General Collins. It was chaotic.

Shots were fired, General Collins and Conrad were yelling.

Then...

Squeal.

It was long and screaming, and when I heard it, I saw it.

Human features but almost reptilian. It was on the screen for a second, then blood splatter with the sound of a shot. The blood covered half of the camera's view on General Collins' side, which told me he was the one that killed it.

The steady automatic weapon firing continued, I watched one of them scurry away. It was large, but thin with long lanky arms he used to move at the same time as his legs.

"I can't. I can't watch anymore." I stood and turned my back.

Every shot, every squeal, yell of our men went through my being. I just couldn't look at the screen anymore. It was like watching a movie so suspenseful you wanted to fast forward.

"There's too many," Conrad called out. "Keep them back. I have to hit the silo."

That was the last resort and not the easy option.

I knew Sam, Jake, and I were safe no matter what happened, but the others... The people out there had no idea what was going on.

"So many. Too many. I got this. Go. Go," Conrad's voice came though broken up.

At that point I looked and my heart sunk.

On General Collins' side all I saw was those things. A force of them like a plague raging toward him.

"Oh my god," I gasped.

With even more gunfire, General Collins' camera flew up in the air and landed from what I could see, on the ground.

Mr. Mosley lowered his head.

It was too much to handle. The view from General Collins side was nothing but the ground. Gunfire rang out and that gave me some hope.

On Conrad's side he ran.

"He made it," Mr. Mosley said. "That's a silo."

Conrad looked behind him and climbed down, he kept looking up. The. Right opening from topside was getting farther away.

Down to the darkness then he'd look back up to the light.

The fourth time he looked up one of those things squealed. It's a team was loud in the hollow silo and it leapt down at Conrad.

There was a shot. A single shot and the cameras went out.

"No, no, no," I whimpered and checked out the time. "There's three minutes left."

"Come in." Mr. Mosley grabbed my hand pulling me with him. I knew where we were going, where we were headed. The only place where we could find out if Conrad had failed or succeeded.

We weren't allowed in there.

Mr. Mosley ran, pulling me along and he didn't wait for the guards, he barged into the room.

It was a tense moment. No one turned around to tell us to leave.

Senator Mitchel stared at the huge radar map. And to my surprise, the president stood off to the side.

"We lost the cameras," said Mr. Mosley.

"Us as well," Senator Mitchell replied.

"Did he do it?" I asked.

"We'll know in twenty seconds." Senator Mitchell looked up.

A red digital timer counted down on the wall.

Fifteen.

Fourteen.

The president looked at me. "It will be fine. We have this. It'll be fine."

Ten.

My eyes shifted from the timer to the radar map. If he failed and the weapon launched, we would see the rocket.

Five.

"Buckle us down," ordered Senator Mitchell. "Just in case."

Three.

Two.

One.

I held my breath. Eyes glued to the screen I was afraid to breathe.

Nothing.

The president held up his hand. "Let's not celebrate yet. Give it a minute."

I wanted to celebrate but he was right. There could be a delay.

I silence we all stood. I reached over grabbing Mr. Mosley's arm.

Waiting.

Waiting.

Minutes that seemed like hours went by.

Then…static.

"He did it," General Collins' voice came over the radio as the camera came back. "The threat has been extinguished. All persons accounted for."

For the moment, that blood pumping victory didn't bring cheers. It brought unison sighs of relief and emotional embraces.

It was over.

For the moment.

But it was not done.

THIRTY-THREE
DEBRIEF

General Collins and Barron were my friends. I waited with bated breath to find out if they were okay and alive.

They were. The entire team that had been sent returned with only minor injuries.

Disaster was averted.

It was understandably a little chaotic waiting on their return. Everyone rushed to them as if they were heroes in a movie, but Conrad, even though he literally saved the day, was still the enemy and would be dealt with accordingly.

I heard talk about possibilities about what they would do with him and his remaining men. The soldiers that came from the future, influenced by probes or not, killed half our population if not more.

The UK, Russia, China, Korea, Japan, and India, like us had disabled the probes with the musical weapon. They were rounding up the future soldiers, securing the weapons, the planes and taking everything they could.

What they would do with the ones in their countries, I hadn't learned yet.

I didn't even know what they were going to do with Conrad.

"I'll fight for him," General Collins told me. "He came through to stop this. He did. They have a debriefing with the president here in a little bit."

"I was shocked to see him alive," I replied. "I wish I could talk to him."

"You will."

Out of the corner of my eye, I saw Mr. Mosely and Barron approaching. They looked, for lack of a better word…sneaky.

"Hey." Barron grabbed my hand, speaking secretively. "It's over, I will work on getting your son out of there and I will before the five years."

"Thank you," I replied.

"But first, Conrad is in the debriefing room. Alone. Let's go talk to him."

"For what?" I asked.

Mr. Mosely answered. "I don't know about you, but I have some questions before they lock him up or do whatever."

It was a good idea, I didn't know what they wanted to ask him, but I knew if they had questions, they weren't getting near Conrad for some time.

When the four of us walked into the room, he sat at the head of the table and looked at us with surprise. He needed cleaning up; he had facial wounds that weren't tended to.

Mr. Mosely walked up, placed a hand on his shoulder and gave it a squeeze before he sat down. "Son, I apologize for not believing you. Good job."

"Thank you, sir. I did what I wanted to," Conrad replied. "Almost."

"What now?" General Collins asked.

"Just move forward as best as you can."

"It won't be that easy now, will it?" Mr. Mosely asked. "How many of them are here?"

Conrad shook his head. "I don't know. I didn't know they were sending them. My guess would be more than we saw and you should be prepared."

"They were creatures," I said. "How were they even communicating with you intelligently. I don't get it."

"They aren't the ones we communicate with," Conrad replied. "They were and are their soldiers. They know one thing. Kill."

General Collins sat down. "At least they die as easy as us, but they're fast."

"You've faced them," Conrad said. "That's an advantage."

"Conrad?" I spoke. "Listen, if Barron doesn't break the five-year seal—"

"I will," Barron said.

I continued, "If he doesn't. How does it happen? How are they released?"

"The seal just disintegrates after five years," Conrad replied. "They'll come out."

"I'll get it." Barron pulled out a chair. "We don't have much time. They're coming in to debrief you and decide what to do with you. But I have a burning question. I know you hid the disabling signal in the songs. But why those songs? Do they have meaning? Do they have a message? It is killing me."

I added, "I wanted to figure it out as well, but I give up. Why those songs?"

"You don't know?" Conrad asked. "Sure, you have to know why those songs?"

We all shook our heads.

"I thought for sure as soon as you heard them, you'd know. Barron, your grandfather loved David Bowie."

"Oh my God," I gasped out. "He did. I remember one year he played David Bowie's Christmas album over the music system constantly. How did I not remember that?"

"And General," Conrad looked at him. "You become a vital part of the AAIT defense initiative, but Eve of Destruction is your favorite song."

"Is it?" I asked.

"Well, yes," General Collins replied. "I didn't say anything because I thought it was inappropriate given the circumstances going on."

Barron tossed up his hands. "Okay, so two of the songs mean something, so we should have picked that up. They mean something so it was our message, but that third song. What is it?"

"Your favorite," Conrad replied. "There was a video going around when you were in your sixties dancing to it."

"I never heard it," Barron replied.

"It was a really famous song. You don't know it?" Conrad asked.

"It's catchy," Mr. Mosely stated.

"I like it," Barron added. "I mean I can see it being a favorite."

"It was your wedding song," Conrad said. "You loved it so much."

Barron shook his head, rubbing his chin. "Really? Okay, thinking about it. The words make sense for a wedding song. Never gonna give you up. Never gonna let you down."

Then General Collins partly sang the rest. "Never gonna run around or desert you."

"Again," Mr. Mosely stated. "Catchy."

"Something is off," Conrad stated. "You should know that song. Anyhow before they come in and you leave, there is something. In the case is a photograph. It is a man that will become president," he said. "I know it's hard to believe but he does. He and General Collins devise an idea for a defense in space. It gets shot down. It never happens. For the future of this planet, perhaps now it should."

With an 'Aw,' Mr. Mosely chuckled. "I get what's happening. Again, your artificial intelligence wasn't all that intelligent. You had Barron's age wrong, you came earlier or later than you think you did, you got the date wrong on that song, and I saw that photo. He already is the president. I'm curious as to what year you think it is. Because it's—"

The door to the debriefing room opened and a soldier announced, "Please stand for the President of the United States."

Immediately, I stood as did everyone else.

The president entered with Senator Mitchell. When I had seen him in the war room, he was dressed much more casually. Now the president looked presidential.

"Conrad." The president extended his hand. "Thank you for your service and for what you have done. You've done a great service to this country."

"Thank you, Mr. President," Conrad replied.

"As you know, well, you can't go without facing some sort of consequence for your participation, no matter how small, in the invasion."

"Yes, sir."

The president looked at us four. "All of you, you have my thanks. But I need the room with this man."

"Yes, sir," General Collins saluted and walked to the door.

"Wait," Conrad called out. "Mr. Mosely. You're right. A lot was wrong. What year is it? You were going to say."

"1983," Mr. Mosely replied, then opened the door to leave.

I followed Barron, but stopped. I had to take my moment I had been waiting for. I hurried over to the president. "Just wanted to say it's an honor to meet you. I voted for you, President Reagan."

"Thank you." He warmly grabbed my hand and smiled. "We'll get that other son of yours back. Now go on. Enjoy this victory with everyone else."

It's not every day a person gets to meet the president and under the circumstances, I was honored. I felt bad because I knew he was destined to be remembered as one of the greats, now he would go into the history books in a different way than he was meant to.

He said to enjoy the victory.

But was it?

Those things were still out there. We won the major battle, the one that would lead us eventually to victory. But by a long shot we hadn't won the war. Not yet. We would.

The genius mind of Barron Acker was stumped by the futuristic and alien technology that bound my son and four hundred others in a Washington State bunker.

288

Barron described it as an organic shell that encompassed every inch of that bunker.

No way in.

No way out.

That was his main focus, to crack that shell.

In the interim though, after eight months he was able to crack into the monitoring system and two-way communication was established.

Nearly a year after they took my son, I spoke to him.

I felt the frustration of a mother whose son was falsely imprisoned. He was fine, he knew what was happening, and things were, as he said, 'Okay' in there.

The United States determined that those who were interned by probes along with Conrad would be sentenced to complete the rebuilding. Even though the future soldiers burned the bodies, there were many that remained.

They killed them, they would bury them.

But that was after many of them were assigned to squads to take on the visitors that remained.

It was an extension of the war that lasted a year. We didn't get them all. The visitors that remained went into hiding.

The government vowed to find them.

I hoped they did before they emerged again.

General Collins led the rebuilding project. Of course, places like Kansas City would never be inhabitable again. There were four point six billion people when the invasion happened. Now they estimated there was less than one billion.

Twenty-five percent of what we were. How long would it take for us to build that back up? Would we ever?

After the war with the visitors, it was deemed safe to move about. Jake, Mr. Mosely and I went back to Hawthorne. Our homes were still standing and I was able to get photo albums and other momentums that meant something to me.

They were all I had left of Luke and Cal. My heart would forever be broken by their loss. Knowing that so many other mothers now had empty arms was no consolation.

For as much as I wanted to stay in Hawthorne, it was a dead town. Not even slated for restructuring. General Collins said it would be one day, but no time in the near future.

Jake and I, along with Mr. Mosely, moved to a small town in Washington. Fourteen miles from the bunker. I visited it three times a week, as if it were a grave. Staring at it. Speaking to my son.

Since I left the mountain, I had no way to communicate with him. I received weekly updates from Barron and messages from Sam.

We set up a home in that small town. It was much like Hawthorne, a small community. Only those of us who lived there had moved there because we were refugees.

As soon as they established a grocery store, I took a job there. Jake went to school. A semi-return to normalcy.

All to pass time, all while waiting for Sam.

Barron worked so hard and swore he would crack the shell and would do so before five years.

He did. Eventually. Not as soon as he wanted. At the four years and three months mark, he knew he broke in.

They announced the day they'd lift the veil and so many people were there.

Jake, Mr. Mosely, and I were three of hundreds. Like us, people were waiting for their families. Those inside knew they were being freed.

I knew Barron was nervous, I could see it in his face as he stood with his mobile equipment.

I had confidence and I was right.

There was no visual confirmation of a veil lifting, but moments after Barron announced the shell was down, people started to emerge.

As they wandered out, shielding their eyes from the sunlight, they looked for people they knew. Some were reunited, some were left disappointed and alone.

Sam came out midway the exodus. I had seen him in the surveillance and raced toward him. It was one of the single greatest moments in my life to hold him, touch him and have him back. Like giving birth to him a second time, I felt that overwhelming feeling.

He had grown a couple inches, his shoulders squared off. He went in an eighteen-year-old boy and emerged a man old enough to have a drink.

I swore I wasn't going to let him go or out of my sight. But he was a man now, he had lived for years without us. I was just going to take every moment that I could with him. There was a lot to tell him, a lot he missed. A lot we would never see.

The contents of Conrad's case helped with that. It became a novelty. The case held a lot about a future that would be different. Pictures of different decades and styles.

I didn't understand why women wanted their hair so big, or men made their hair curly.

I never would.

Things were getting back on track. We had utilities, jobs, bills to pay, the price of gas was outrageous once trade opened back up.

It took three years, but it did.

We even had television again. Old programs replayed. Nothing new yet. I didn't see us having those little mobile telephones that Conrad said people couldn't live without. I hoped that was one thing that never happened. From what he told me, they took away the personal connection we all had that made us human.

Although, I was sure the future we were supposed to have was filled with movies and television shows that shaped our world.

Now it was time to recreate them and a new future.

So many people talked about the war and how it fixed things.

They didn't fix anything; they didn't stop it from happening. Winning the war in my opinion made it worse. The technology, the planes, the Artificial Intelligence, everything they brought was now in our hands decades before it should have been.

It was completely in the realm of possibility that they simply jumpstarted the chain of events that would repeat.

Maybe, just maybe we would learn from the mistakes that were made in our future. One thing I knew I learned, I would never make the same fashion and hair mistakes.

What were people thinking?

It would take some time to get back into that carefree mindset we had.

Even years later, even with phones, television, nightly talk shows and shopping, we were still recovering from the war and losses. Learning and moving forward.

My personal vow not to repeat mistakes of those of our future fathers made was miniscule and held no weight against the leaders of the countries that made all the choices. But I was one person in a sea of many.

I could only live the best life I could. Embrace the second chances I was given with my sons and take it all one day at a time.

Jacqueline Druga is a native of Pittsburgh, PA. Her works include genres of all types but she favours post-apocalypse and apocalypse writing.

Follow the author:
Facebook: @jacquelinedruga
Twitter: @gojake
Website: www.jacquelinedruga.com